<u>Georgian</u> <u>Gothic</u>

Short Stories from the Writers of the Finest Gothic and Ghostly Horror

British Library Cataloguing-in-Publication Data
A catalogue record for this book is available from
the British Library

Contents

Selected Biographies of the Authors

THE TRANSFORMATION

Mary Shelley

* * *

'Forthwith this frame of mine was wrench'd
  With a woful agony,
Which forced me to begin my tale,
  And then it set me free.

'Since then, at an uncertain hour,
  That agony returns;
And till my ghastly tale is told
  This heart within me burns.'

—COLERIDGE'S ANCIENT MARINER.

I have heard it said, that, when any strange, supernatural, and necromantic adventure has occurred to a human being, that being, however desirous he may be to conceal the same, feels at certain period torn up as it were by an intellectual earthquake, and is forced to bare the inner depths of his spirit to another. I am a witness of the truth of this. I have dearly sworn to myself never to reveal to human ears the horrors to which I once, in excess of fiendly pride, delivered myself over. The holy man who heard my confession and reconciled me to the Church, is dead. None knows that once—

Why should it not be thus? Why tell a tale of impious tempting of Providence, and soul-subduing humiliation? Why? answer me, ye who are wise in the secrets of human nature! I only know that so it is; and in spite of strong resolve – of a pride that too much masters me – of shame, and even of fear, so to render myself odious to my species – I must speak.

Genoa! my birthplace – proud city! looking upon the blue Mediterranean – dost thou remember me in my boyhood, when thy cliffs and promontories, thy bright sky and gay vineyards, were my world? Happy time! when to the young heart the narrow-bounded universe, which leaves, by its very limitation, free scope to the imagination, enchains our physical energies, and, sole period in our lives, innocence and enjoyment are united. Yet, who can look back to childhood, and not remember its sorrows and its harrowing fears? I was born with the most imperious, haughty, tameless spirit. I quailed before my father only; and he, generous and noble, but capricious and tyrannical, at once fostered and checked the wild impetuosity of my character, making obedience necessary, but inspiring no respect for the motives which guided his commands. To be a man, free, independent; or, in better words, insolent and domineering, was the hope and prayer of my rebel heart.

My father had one friend, a wealthy Genoese noble, who in a political tumult was suddenly sentenced to banishment, and his property confiscated. The Marchese Torella went into exile alone. Like my father, he was a widower: he had one child, the almost infant Juliet, who was left under my father's guardianship. I should certainly have been unkind to the lovely girl, but that I was forced by my position to become her protector. A variety of childish incidents all tended to one point – to make Juliet see in me a rock of defence; I in her, one who must perish through the soft sensibility of her nature too rudely visited, but for my guardian care. We grew up together. The opening rose in May was not more sweet than this dear girl. An irradiation of beauty was spread over her face. Her form, her step, her voice – my heart weeps even now, to think of all the gentleness, loving and pure, that she enshrined. When I was eleven, and Juliet eight years of age, a cousin of mine, much older than either – he seemed to us a man – took great notice of my playmate;

he called her his bride, and asked her to marry him. She refused, and he insisted, drawing her unwillingly towards him. With the countenance and emotions of a maniac, I threw myself on him – I strove to draw his sword – I clung to his neck with the ferocious resolve to strangle him; he was obliged to call for assistance to disengage himself from me. On that night I led Juliet to the chapel of our house: I made her touch the sacred relics – I harrowed her child's heart, and profaned her child's lips with an oath, that she would be mine and mine only.

Well, those days passed away. Torella returned in a few years, and became wealthier and more prosperous than ever. When I was seventeen, my father died; he had been magnificent to prodigality; Torella rejoiced that my minority would afford an opportunity for repairing my fortunes. Juliet and I had been affianced beside my father's deathbed – Torella was to be a second parent to me.

I desired to see the world, and I was indulged. I went to Florence, to Rome, to Naples; thence I passed to Toulon, and at length reached what had long been the bourne of my wishes, Paris. There was wild work in Paris then. The poor king, Charles the Sixth, now sane, now mad, now a monarch, now an abject slave, was the very mockery of humanity. The queen, the dauphin, the Duke of Burgundy, alternately friends and foes – now meeting in prodigal feasts, now shedding blood in rivalry – were blind to the miserable state of their country, and the dangers that impended over it, and gave themselves wholly up to dissolute enjoyment or savage strife. My character still followed me. I was arrogant and self-willed; I loved display, and above all, I threw off all control. My young friends were eager to foster passions which furnished them with pleasures. I was deemed handsome – I was master of every knightly accomplishment. I was disconnected with any political party. I grew a favourite with all: my presumption and arrogance was pardoned in one so young: I became a spoiled child. Who could control me? not the letters and advice of Torella – only strong necessity visiting me in the abhorred shape of an empty purse. But there were means to refill this void. Acre after acre, estate after estate, I sold. My dress, my jewels, my horses and their caparisons, were almost unrivalled in gorgeous Paris, while the lands of my inheritance passed into possession of others.

The Duke of Orleans was waylaid and murdered by the Duke of Burgundy. Fear and terror possessed all Paris. The dauphin and the queen shut themselves up; every pleasure was suspended. I grew weary of this state of things, and my heart yearned for my boyhood's haunts. I was nearly a beggar, yet still I would go there, claim my bride, and rebuild my fortunes. A few happy ventures as a merchant would make me rich again. Nevertheless, I would not return in humble guise. My last act was to dispose of my remaining estate near Albaro for half its worth, for ready money. Then I despatched all kinds of artificers, arras, furniture of regal splendour, to fit up the last relic of my inheritance, my palace in Genoa. I lingered a little longer yet, ashamed at the part of the prodigal returned, which I feared I should play. I sent my horses. One matchless Spanish jennet I despatched to my promised bride: its caparisons flamed with jewels and cloth of gold. In every part I caused to be entwined the initials of Juliet and her Guido. My present found favour in hers and in her father's eyes.

Still to return a proclaimed spendthrift, the mark of impertinent wonder, perhaps of scorn, and to encounter singly the reproaches or taunts of my fellow-citizens, was no alluring prospect. As a shield between me and censure, I invited some few of the most reckless of my comrades to accompany me: thus I went armed against the world, hiding a rankling feeling, half fear and half penitence, by bravado.

I arrived in Genoa. I trod the pavement of my ancestral palace. My proud step was no interpreter of my heart, for I deeply felt that, though surrounded by every luxury, I was a beggar. The first step I took in claiming Juliet must widely declare me such. I read contempt or pity in the looks of all. I fancied that rich and poor, young and old, all regarded me with derision. Torella came not near me. No wonder that my second father should expect a son's deference from me in waiting first on him. But, galled and stung by a sense of my follies and demerit, I strove to throw the blame on others. We kept nightly orgies in Palazzo Carega. To sleepless, riotous nights followed listless, supine mornings. At the Ave Maria we showed our dainty persons in the streets, scoffing at the sober citizens, casting insolent glances on the shrinking women. Juliet was not among them – no, no; if she had been there, shame would have driven me away, if love had not brought me to her feet.

I grew tired of this. Suddenly I paid the Marchese a visit. He was at his villa, one among the many which deck the suburb of San Pietro d'Arena. It was the month of May, the blossoms of the fruit-trees were fading among thick, green foliage; the vines were shooting forth; the ground strewed with the fallen olive blooms; the firefly was in the myrtle hedge; heaven and earth wore a mantle of surpassing beauty. Torella welcomed me kindly, though seriously; and even his shade of displeasure soon wore away. Some resemblance to my father – some look and tone of youthful ingenuousness, softened the good old man's heart. He sent for his daughter – he presented me to her as her betrothed. The chamber became hallowed by a holy light as she entered. Hers was that cherub look, those large, soft eyes, full dimpled cheeks, and mouth of infantine sweetness, that expresses the rare union of happiness and love. Admiration first possessed me; she is mine! was the second proud emotion, and my lips curled with haughty triumph. I had not been the *enfant gâté* of the beauties of France not to have learnt the art of pleasing the soft heart of woman. If towards men I was overbearing, the deference I paid to them was the more in contrast. I commenced my courtship by the display of a thousand gallantries to Juliet, who, vowed to me from infancy, had never admitted the devotion of others; and who, though accustomed to expressions of admiration, was uninitiated in the language of lovers.

For a few days all went well. Torella never alluded to my extravagance; he treated me as a favourite son. But the time came, as we discussed the preliminaries to my union with his daughter, when this fair face of things should be overcast. A contract had been drawn up in my father's lifetime. I had rendered this, in fact, void, by having squandered the whole of the wealth which was to have been shared by Juliet and myself. Torella, in consequence, chose to consider this bond as cancelled, and proposed another, in which, though the wealth he bestowed was immeasurably increased, there were so many restrictions as to the mode of spending it, that I, who saw independence only in free career being given to my own imperious will, taunted him as taking advantage of my situation, and refused utterly to subscribe to his conditions. The old man mildly strove to recall me to reason. Roused pride became the tyrant of my thought: I listened with indignation – I repelled him with disdain.

'Juliet, thou art mine! Did we not interchange vows in our innocent childhood? Are we not one in the sight of God? And shall thy cold-hearted, cold-blooded father divide us? Be generous, my love, be just; take not away a gift, last treasure of thy Guido – retract not thy vows – let us defy the world, and setting at nought the calculations of age, find in our mutual affection a refuge from every ill.'

Fiend I must have been with such sophistry to endeavour to poison that sanctuary of holy thought and tender love. Juliet shank from me affrighted. Her father was the best and kindest of men, and she strove to show me how, in obeying him, every good would follow. He would receive my tardy submission with warm affection, and generous pardon would follow my repentance – profitless words for a young and gentle daughter to use to a man accustomed to make his will law, and to feel in his own heart a despot so terrible and stern that he could yield obedience to nought save his own imperious desires! My resentment grew with resistance; my wild companions were ready to add fuel to the flame. We laid a plan to carry off Juliet. At first it appeared to be crowned with success. Midway, on our return, we were overtaken by the agonized father and his attendants. A conflict ensued. Before the city guard came to decide the victory in favour of our antagonists, two of Torella's servitors were dangerously wounded.

This portion of my history weighs most heavily with me. Changed man as I am, I abhor myself in the recollection. May none who hear this tale ever have felt as I. A horse driven to fury by a rider armed with barbed spurs was not more a slave than I to the violent tyranny of my temper. A fiend possessed my soul, irritating it to madness. I felt the voice of conscience within me; but if I yielded to it for a brief interval, it was only to be a moment after torn, as by a whirlwind, away – borne along on the stream of desperate rage – the plaything of the storms engendered by pride. I was imprisoned, and, at the instance of Torella, set free. Again I returned to carry off both him and his child to France, which hapless country, then preyed on by freebooters and gangs of lawless soldiery, offered a grateful refuge to a criminal like me. Our plots were discovered. I was sentenced to banishment; and, as my debts were already enormous, my remaining property was put in the hands of commissioners for their payment. Torella again offered his mediation, requiring only my promise not to renew my abortive attempts on himself and his daughter. I spurned his offers, and fancied that I triumphed when I was thrust out from Genoa, a solitary and penniless exile. My companions were gone: they had been dismissed the city some weeks before, and were already in France. I was alone – friendless, with neither sword at my side, nor ducat in my purse.

I wandered along the seashore, a whirlwind of passion possessing and tearing my soul. It was as if a live coal had been set burning in my breast. At first I meditated on what I should do. I would join a band of freebooters. Revenge! – the word seemed balm to me; I hugged it, caressed it, till, like a serpent, it stung me. Then again I would abjure and despise Genoa, that little corner of the world. I would return to Paris, where so many of my friends swarmed; where my services would be eagerly accepted; where I would carve out fortune with my sword, and make my paltry birthplace and the false Torella rue the day when they drove me, a new Coriolanus, from her walls. I would return to Paris – thus on foot – a beggar – and present myself in my poverty to those I had formerly entertained sumptuously? There was gall in the mere thought of it.

The reality of things began to dawn upon my mind, bringing despair in its train. For several months I had been a prisoner: the evils of my dungeon had whipped my soul to madness, but they had subdued my corporeal frame. I was weak and wan. Torella had used a thousand artifices to administer to my comfort; I had detected and scorned them all, and I reaped the harvest of my obduracy. What was to be done? Should I crouch before my foe, and sue for forgiveness? – Die rather ten thousand deaths! – Never should they obtain that victory! Hate – I swore eternal hate! Hate from whom? – to whom? – From a wandering outcast – to a mighty noble! I and my feelings were nothing to them: already had they forgotten one so unworthy. And Juliet! – her angel face and sylph-like form gleamed among the clouds of my despair with vain beauty; for I had lost her – the glory and flower of the world! Another will call her his! – that smile of paradise will bless another!

Even now my heart fails within me when I recur to this rout of grim-visaged ideas. Now subdued almost to tears, now raving in my agony, still I wandered along the rocky shore, which grew at each step wilder and more desolate. Hanging rocks and hoar precipices overlooked the tideless ocean; black caverns yawned; and for ever, among the sea-worn recesses, murmured and washed the unfruitful waters. Now my way was almost barred by an abrupt promontory, now rendered nearly impracticable by fragments fallen from the cliff. Evening was at hand, when, seaward, arose, as if on the waving of a wizard's wand, a murky web of clouds, blotting the late azure sky, and darkening and disturbing the till now placid deep. The clouds had strange, fantastic shapes, and they changed and mingled and seemed to be driven about by a mighty spell. The waves raised their white crests; the thunder first muttered, then roared from across the waste of waters, which took a deep purple dye, flecked with foam. The spot where I stood looked, on one side, to the widespread ocean; on the other, it was barred by a rugged promontory. Round this cape suddenly came, driven by the wind, a vessel. In vain the mariners tried to force a path for her to the open sea – the gale drove her on the rocks. It will perish! – all on board will perish! Would I were among them! And to my young heart the idea of death came for the first time blended with that of joy. It was an awful sight to behold that vessel struggling with her fate. Hardly could I discern the sailors, but I heard them. It was soon all over! A rock, just covered by the tossing waves, and so unperceived, lay in wait for its prey. A crash of thunder broke over my head at the moment that, with a frightful shock, the vessel dashed upon her unseen enemy. In a brief space of time she went to pieces. There I stood in safety; and there were my fellow-creatures battling, how hopelessly, with annihilation. Methought I saw them struggling – too truly did I hear their shrieks, conquering the barking surges in their shrill agony. The dark breakers threw hither and thither the fragments of the wreck: soon it disappeared. I had been fascinated to gaze till the end: at last I sank on my knees – I covered my face with my hands. I again looked up; something was floating on the billows towards the shore. It neared and neared. Was that a human form? It grew more and more distinct; and at last a mighty wave, lifting the whole freight, lodged it upon a rock. A human being bestriding a sea-chest! – a human being! Yet was it one? Surely never such had existed before – a misshapen dwarf, with squinting eyes, distorted features, and body deformed, till it became a horror to behold. My blood, lately warming towards a fellow-being so snatched from a watery tomb, froze in my heart. The dwarf got off his chest; he tossed his straight, struggling hair from his odious visage.

'By St. Beelzebub!' he exclaimed, 'I have been well bested.' He looked round and saw me. 'Oh, by the fiend! here is another ally of the mighty One. To what saint did you offer prayers, friend – if not to mine? Yet I remember you not on board.'

I shrank from the monster and his blasphemy. Again he questioned me, and I muttered some inaudible reply. He continued:

'Your voice is drowned by this dissonant roar. What a noise the big ocean makes! Schoolboys bursting from their prison are not louder than these waves set free to play. They disturb me. I will no more of their ill-timed brawling. Silence, hoary One! – Winds, avaunt! – to your homes! – Clouds, fly to the antipodes, and leave our heaven clear!'

As he spoke, he stretched out his two long, lank arms, that looked like spider's claws, and seemed to embrace with them the expanse before him. Was it a miracle? The clouds became broken and fled; the azure sky first peeped out, and then was spread a calm field of blue above us; the stormy gale was exchanged to the softly breathing west; the sea grew calm; the waves dwindled to riplets.

'I like obedience even in these stupid elements,' said the dwarf. 'How much more in the tameless mind of man! It was a well-got-up storm, you must allow – and all of my own making.'

It was tempting Providence to interchange talk with this magician. But *Power* in all its shapes, is respected by man. Awe, curiosity, a clinging fascination, drew me towards him.

'Come, don't be frightened, friend,' said the wretch: 'I am good humoured when pleased; and something does please me in your well-proportioned body and handsome face, though you look a little woe-begone. You have suffered a land – I, a sea wreck. Perhaps I can allay the tempest of your fortunes as I did my own. Shall we be friends!' – And he held out his hand; I could not touch it. 'Well, then, companions – that will do as well. And now, while I rest after the buffeting I underwent just now, tell me why, young and gallant as you seem, you wander thus alone and downcast as this wild seashore.'

The voice of the wretch was screeching and horrid, and his contortions as he spoke were frightful to behold. Yet he did gain a kind of influence over me, which I could not master; and I told him my tale. When it was ended, he laughed long and loud: the rocks echoed back the sound: hell seemed yelling around me.

'Oh, thou cousin of Lucifer!' said he; 'so thou too hast fallen through thy pride; and, though bright as the son of Morning, thou art ready to give up thy good looks, thy bride, and thy well-being, rather than submit thee to the tyranny of good. I honour thy choice, by my soul! – So thou hast fled, and yield the day; and mean to starve on these rocks, and to let the birds peck out thy dead eyes, while thy enemy and thy betrothed rejoice in thy ruin. Thy pride is strangely akin to humility, methinks.'

As he spoke, a thousand fanged thoughts stung me to the heart.

'What would you that I should do?' I cried.

'I! – Oh, nothing, but lie down and say your prayers before you die. But, were I you, I know the deed that should be done.'

I drew near him. His supernatural powers made him an oracle in my eyes; yet a strange unearthly thrill quivered through my frame as I said, 'Speak! – teach me – what act do you advise?'

'Revenge thyself, man! – humble thy enemies! – set thy foot on the old man's neck, and possess thyself of his daughter!'

'To the east and west I turn,' cried I, 'and see no means! Had I gold, much could I achieve; but, poor and single, I am powerless.'

The dwarf had been seated on his chest as he listened to my story. Now he got off; he touched a spring; it flew open! What a mine of wealth – of blazing jewels, beaming gold, and pale silver – was displayed therein. A mad desire to possess this treasure was born within me.

'Doubtless,' I said, 'one so powerful as you could do all things.'

'Nay,' said the monster humbly, 'I am less omnipotent than I seem. Some things I possess which you may covet; but I would give them all for a small share, or even for a loan of what is yours.'

'My possessions are at your service,' I replied bitterly – 'my poverty, my exile, my disgrace – I make a free gift of them all.'

'Good! I thank you. Add one other thing to your gift, and my treasure is yours.'

'As nothing is my sole inheritance, what besides nothing would you have?'

'Your comely face and well-made limbs.'

I shivered. Would this all-powerful monster murder me? I had no dagger. I forgot to pray – but I grew pale.

'I ask for a loan, not a gift,' said the frightful thing: 'lend me your body for three days – you shall have mine to cage your soul the while, and, in payment, my chest. What say you to the bargain? – Three short days.'

We are told that it is dangerous to hold unlawful talk; and well do I prove the same. Tamely written down, it may seem incredible that I should lend any ear to this proposition; but, in spite of his unnatural ugliness, there was something fascinating in a being whose voice could govern earth, air, and sea. I felt a keen desire to comply; for with that chest I could command the world. My only hesitation resulted from a fear that he would not be true to his bargain. Then, I thought, I shall soon die here on these lonely sands, and the limbs he covets will be mine no more – it is worth the chance. And, besides, I knew that, by all the rules of art-magic, there were formulas and oaths which none of its practisers dared break. I hesitated to reply; and he went on, now displaying his wealth, now speaking of the petty price he demanded, till it seemed madness to refuse. Thus is it – place our bark in the current of the stream, and down, over fall and cataract it is hurried; give up our conduct to the wild torrent of passion, and we are away, we know not whither.

He swore many an oath, and I adjured him by many a

sacred name; till I saw this wonder of power, this ruler of the elements, shiver like an autumn leaf before my words; and as if the spirit spake unwillingly and perforce within him, at last, he, with broken voice, revealed the spell whereby he might be obliged, did he wish to play me false, to render up the unlawful spoil. Our warm life-blood must mingle to make and to mar the charm.

Enough of this unholy theme. I was persuaded – the thing was done. The morrow dawned upon me as I lay upon the shingles, and I knew not my own shadow as it fell from me. I felt myself changed to a shape of horror, and cursed my easy faith and blind credulity. The chest was there – there the gold and precious stones for which I had sold the frame of flesh which nature had given me. The sight a little stilled my emotions: three days would soon be gone.

They did pass. The dwarf had supplied me with a plenteous store of food. At first I could hardly walk, so strange and out of joint were all my limbs; and my voice – it was that of the fiend. But I kept silent, and turned my face to the sun, that I might not see my shadow, and counted the hours, and ruminated on my future conduct. To bring Torella to my feet – to possess my Juliet in spite of him – all this my wealth could easily achieve. During dark night I slept, and dreamt of the accomplishment of my desires. Two suns had set – the third dawned. I was agitated, fearful. Oh expectation, what a frightful thing art thou, when kindled more by fear than hope! How dost thou twist thyself round the heart, torturing its pulsations! How dost thou dart unknown pangs all through our feeble mechanism, now seeming to shiver us like broken glass, to nothingness – now giving us a fresh strength, which can *do* nothing, and so torments us by a sensation, such as the strong man must feel who cannot break his fetters, though they bend in his grasp. Slowly paced the bright, bright orb up the eastern sky; long it lingered in the zenith, and still more slowly wandered down the west: it touched the horizon's verge – it was lost! Its glories were on the summits of the cliff – they grew dun and grey. The evening star shone bright. He will soon be here.

He came not! – By the living heavens, he came not! – and night dragged out its weary length, and, in its decaying age, 'day began to grizzle its dark hair'; and the sun rose again on the most miserable wretch that ever upbraided its light. Three days thus I passed. The jewels and the gold – oh, how I abhorred them!

Well, well – I will not blacken these pages with demoniac ravings. All too terrible were the thoughts, the raging tumult of ideas that filled my soul. At the end of that time I slept; I had not before since the third sunset; and I dreamt that I was at Juliet's feet, and she smiled, and then she shrieked – for she saw my transformation – and again she smiled, for still her beautiful lover knelt before her. But it was not I – it was he, the fiend, arrayed in my limbs, speaking with my voice, winning her with my looks of love. I strove to warn her, but my tongue refused its office; I strove to tear him from her, but I was rooted to the ground – I awoke with the agony. There were the solitary hoar precipices – there the splashing sea, the quiet strand and the blue sky over all. What did it mean? Was my dream but a mirror of the truth? Was he wooing and winning my betrothed? I would on the instant back to Genoa – but I was banished. I laughed – the dwarf's yell burst from my lips – I banished! Oh no! they had not exiled the foul limbs I wore; I might with these enter, without fear of incurring the threatened penalty of death, my own, my native city.

I began to walk towards Genoa. I was somewhat accustomed to my distorted limbs; none were ever so ill-adapted for a straightforward movement; it was with infinite difficulty that I proceeded. Then, too, I desired to avoid all hamlets strewed here and there on the sea-beach, for I was unwilling to make a display of my hideousness. I was not quite sure that, if seen, the mere boys would not stone me to death as I passed, for a monster; some ungentle salutations I did receive from the few peasants or fishermen I chanced to meet. But it was dark night before I approached Genoa. The weather was so balmy and sweet that it struck me that the Marchese and his daughter would very probably have quitted the city for their country retreat. It was from Villa Torella that I had attempted to carry off Juliet; I had spent many an hour reconnoitring the spot, and knew each inch of ground in its vicinity. It was beautifully situated, embosomed in trees, on the margin of a stream. As I drew near, it became evident that my conjecture was right; nay, moreover, that the hours were being then devoted to feasting and merriment. For the house was lighted up; strains of soft and gay music were wafted towards me by the breeze. My heart sank within me. Such was the generous kindness of Torella's heart that I felt sure that he would not have indulged in public manifestations of rejoicing just after my unfortunate banishment, but for a cause I dared not dwell upon.

The country people were all alive and flocking about; it became necessary that I should conceal myself; and yet I longed to address someone, or to hear others discourse, or in any way to gain intelligence of what was really going on. At length, entering the walks that were in immediate vicinity to the mansion, I found one dark enough to veil my excessive frightfulness; and yet others as well as I were loitering in its shade. I soon gathered all I wanted to know – all that first made my very heart die with horror, and then boil with indignation. Tomorrow Juliet was to be given to the penitent, reformed, beloved Guido – tomorrow my bride was to pledge her vows to a fiend from hell! And I did this! – my accursed pride – my demoniac violence and wicked self-idolatry had caused this act. For if I had acted as the wretch who had stolen my form had acted – if, with a mien at once yielding and dignified, I had presented myself to Torella, saying, I have done wrong, forgive me; I am unworthy of your angel-child, but permit me to claim her hereafter, when my altered conduct shall manifest that I abjure my vices, and endeavour to become in some sort worthy of her. I go to serve against the infidels; and when my zeal for religion and my true penitence for the past shall appear to you to cancel my crimes, permit me again to call myself your son. Thus had he spoken; and the penitent was welcomed even as the prodigal son of Scripture: the fatted calf was killed for him; and he, still pursuing the same path, displayed such open-hearted regret for his follies, so humble a concession of all his rights, and so ardent a resolve to reacquire them by a life of contrition and virtue, that he quickly conquered the kind old man, and full pardon, and the gift of his lovely child, followed in swift succession.

Oh, had an angel from Paradise whispered to me to act thus! But now, what would be the innocent Juliet's fate? Would God permit the foul union – or, some prodigy destroying it, link the dishonoured name of Carega with the worst of crimes? Tomorrow at dawn they were to be married: there was but one way to prevent this – to meet mine enemy, and to enforce the ratification of our agreement. I felt that this could only be done by a mortal struggle. I had no sword – if indeed my distorted arms could wield a soldier's weapon – but I had a dagger, and in that lay my hope. There was no time for pondering or balancing nicely the question: I might die in the attempt; but besides the burning jealousy and despair of my own heart, honour, mere humanity, demanded that I should fall rather than not destroy the machinations of the fiend.

The guests departed – the lights began to disappear; it was evident that the inhabitants of the villa were seeking repose. I hid myself among the trees – the garden grew desert – the gates were closed – I wandered round and came under a window – ah! well did I know the same! – a soft twilight glimmered in the room – the curtains were half withdrawn. It was the temple of innocence and beauty. Its magnificence was tempered, as it were, by the slight disarrangements occasioned by its being dwelt in, and all the objects scattered around displayed the taste of her who hallowed it by her presence. I saw her enter with a quick light step – I saw her approach the window – she drew back the curtain yet further, and looked out into the night. Its breezy freshness played among her ringlets, and wafted them from the transparent marble of her brow. She clasped her hands, she raised her eyes to heaven. I heard her voice. Guido! she softly murmured – mine own Guido! and then, as if overcome by the fullness of her own heart, she sank on her knees – her up-raised eyes – her graceful attitude – the beaming thank-fulness that lighted up her face – oh, these are tame words! Heart of mine, thou imagest ever, though thou canst not portray, the celestial beauty of that child of light and love.

I heard a step – a quick firm step along the shady avenue. Soon I saw a cavalier, richly dressed, young and, methought, graceful to look on, advance. I hid myself yet closer. The youth approached; he paused beneath the window. She arose, and again looking out she saw him, and said – I cannot, no, at this distant time I cannot record her terms of soft silver tenderness; to me they were spoken, but they were replied to by him.

'I will not go,' he cried: 'here where you have been, where your memory glides like some heaven-visiting ghost, I will pass the long hours till we meet, never, my Juliet, again, day or night, to part. But do thou, my love, retire; the cold morn and fitful breeze will make thy cheek pale, and fill with languor thy love-lighted eyes. Ah, sweetest! could I press one kiss upon them, I could, methinks repose.'

And then he approached still nearer, and methought he was about to clamber into her chamber. I had hesitated, not to terrify her; now I was no longer master of myself. I rushed forward – I threw myself on him – I tore him away – I cried, 'O loathsome and foul-shaped wretch!'

I need not repeat epithets, all tending, as it appeared, to rail at a person I at present feel some partiality for. A shriek rose from Juliet's lips. I neither heard nor saw – I *felt* only mine enemy, whose throat I grasped, and my dagger's hilt; he struggled, but could not escape. At length hoarsely he breathed these words: 'Do! – strike home! destroy this body – you will still live: may your life be long and merry!'

The descending dagger was arrested at the word, and he, feeling my hold relax, extricated himself and drew his sword, while the uproar in the house, and flying of torches from one room to the other, showed that soon we should be separated. In the midst of my frenzy there was much calculation – fall I might, and so that he did not survive I cared not for the death-blow I might deal against myself. While still, therefore, he thought I paused, and while I saw the villainous resolve to take advantage of my hesitation, in the sudden thrust he made at me, I threw myself on his sword, and at the same moment plunged my dagger, with a true, desperate aim, in his side. We fell together, rolling over each other, and the tide of blood that flowed from the gaping wound of each mingled on the grass. More I know not – I fainted.

Again I return to life: weak almost to death, I found myself stretched upon a bed – Juliet was kneeling beside it. Strange! my first broken request was for a mirror. I was so wan and ghastly, that my poor girl hesitated, as she told me afterwards; but, by the mass! I thought myself a right proper youth when I saw the dear reflection of my own well-known features. I confess it is a weakness, but I avow it, I do entertain a considerable affection for the countenance and limbs I behold, whenever I look at a glass; and have more mirrors in my house, and consult them oftener, than any beauty in Genoa. Before you too much condemn me, permit me to say that no one better knows than I the value of his own body; no one, probably except myself, ever having had it stolen from him.

Incoherently I at first talked of the dwarf and his crimes, and reproached Juliet for her too easy admission of his love. She thought me raving, as well she might; and yet it was some time before I could prevail on myself to admit that the Guido whose penitence had won her back for me was myself; and while I cursed bitterly the monstrous dwarf, and blest the well-directed blow that had deprived him of life, I suddenly checked myself when I heard her say, Amen! knowing that him whom she reviled was my very self. A little reflection taught me silence – a little practice enabled me to speak of that frightful night without any excessive blunder. The wound I had given myself was no mockery of one – it was long before I recovered – and as the benevolent and generous Torella sat beside me, talking such wisdom as might win friends to repentance, and mine own dear Juliet hovered near me, administering to my wants, and cheering me by her smiles, the work of my bodily cure and mental reform went on together. I have never, indeed, wholly recovered my strength – my cheek is paler since – my person a little bent. Juliet sometimes ventures to allude bitterly to the malice that caused this change, but I kiss her on the moment, and tell her all is for the best. I am a fonder and more faithful husband, and true is this – but for that wound, never had I called her mine.

I did not revisit the seashore, nor seek for the fiend's treasure; yet, while I ponder on the past, I often think, and my confessor was not backward in favouring the idea, that it might be a good rather than an evil spirit, sent by my guardian angel, to show me the folly and misery of pride. So well at least did I learn this lesson, roughly taught as I was, that I am known now by all my friends and fellow-citizens by the name of Guido il Cortese.

THE THREE LOW MASSES

Alphonse Daudet

'Two stuffed turkeys, Garrigou?'

'Yes, Father, two magnificent turkeys stuffed with truffles. And I ought to know, too, for I helped stuff them myself. One would think their skins would crack while they were roasting, they are stretched so tight.'

'Jesus and Mary! I who love truffles so much! . . . Quick, Garrigou, give me my surplice . . . And besides the turkey, what else did you see in the kitchens?'

'Oh, all sorts of good things! Ever since noon we have been plucking pheasants, hoopoes, hazel-lens and heath-cocks. The feathers filled with air. And then from the pond they brought eels, goldfish, trout, and . . .'

'How big were the trout, Garrigou?'

'So big, Father! Enormous!'

'Oh, good Lord! I can fairly see them . . . Did you put the wine in the vases?'

'Yes, Father, I put the wine in the vases. But heavens! It's nothing like the wine you will have later, when you come from the midnight mass. Oh, if you could only see the dining hall, all the decanters blazing with wines of all colours! And the silverware, the chased centrepieces, the flowers the candelabra! Never was there seen such a Christmas feast! The marquis has invited all the lords of the neighbouring estates. There will be at least forty of you at the table, without counting the bailiff or the notary. Ah! you are fortunate in being one of them, Father! Only from sniffing those wonderful turkeys, the odour of truffles follows me everywhere. Mmmm!'

'Come, come, my boy! Heaven preserve us from the sin of gluttony, above all on this eve of the Nativity! . . . Hurry off, now, and light the tapers and ring the first call for mass, for it will soon be midnight and we mustn't be late.'

This conversation took place one Christmas Eve in the year of grace sixteen hundred and something, between the Reverend Dom Balaguere, former prior of the Barnabites and present chaplain of the Sires of Trinquelage, and his little clerk Garrigou—or at least him whom he believed to be the little clerk Garrigou, for let me tell you that the devil, that evening, had assumed the round face and uncertain features of the young sacristan, the better to lead the reverend Father into temptation and make him commit the frightful sin of gluttony. So while the so-called Garrigou (hm! hm!) rang out the chimes from the seigniorial chapel, the reverend Father slipped on his chasuble in the little vestry of the castle, and, his imagination already excited by Garrigou's gastronomical descriptions, he kept muttering to himself as he got into his vestments:

'Roast turkeys . . . goldfish . . . trout, so big!'

Outside, the night wind blew and spread abroad the music of the bells. Lights began to appear in the darkness on the sides of Mount Ventoux, on whose summit the old towers of Trinquelage upreared their heads. The neighbouring farmers and their families were on their way to the castle to hear midnight mass. They climbed the mountain singing gaily, in groups of five or six, the father leading the way with his lantern, the women following, wrapped in great dark coats, under which the children snuggled to keep warm. In spite of the cold and the late hour of the night, all these good people walked along merrily, cheered by the thought that on coming from the mass they would find as usual, a great feast awaiting them downstairs in the castle kitchen. From time to time, on the rough ascent, the carriage of some lord, preceded by torch-bearers, showed its glimmering windowpanes in the moonlight; or a mule trotted along shaking its bells; or again, by the gleam of the great lanterns wrapped in mist, the farmers recognised their bailiff and hailed him as he passed:

'Good evening, good evening, Master Arnoton!'

'Good evening, good evening, my children!'

The night was clear; the stars seemed brightened by the frost; the northeast wind was nipping; and a fine sleet powdered all these cloaks without wetting them, preserving faithfully the tradition of a Christmas white with snow. On the very crest of the mountain the castle appeared as the goal, with its huge mass of towers and gables, the chapel steeple rising straight into the blue-black sky, and a crowd of little lights moving rapidly hither and thither, winking at all the windows, and looking, against the intense black of that lordly pile, like the little sparks that run through the ashes of burnt paper.

After passing the drawbridge and the postern, in order to get to the chapel one had to cross the first court, full of coaches, footmen and sedan-chairs silhouetted against the flare of the torches and the glare from the kitchens. One could hear the creaking of the turning spits, the clatter of pots, the tinkling of glassware and silver, as they were laid out for the banquet; and above it all floated a warm vapour smelling of roasted meats and the pungent herbs of elaborate sauces, which made the farmers, as well as the chaplain, the bailiff, and everybody say:

'What a wonderful midnight feast we are going to have after the mass!'

*　　*　　*

Ding-a-ling-ling! Ding-a-ling-ling! The midnight mass has begun. In the chapel of the castle, which is a miniature cathedral with its inter-crossed arches and oaken wainscoting up to the ceiling, all the tapestries are hung, all the tapers lighted. What a crowd of people! And what sumptuous costumes! Here, in one of the carven stalls that surround the choir, is the Sire of Trinquelage, clad in salmon-coloured silk; and around him all the noble lords, his guests. Opposite them, on velvet fall-stools, kneel the old dowager marchioness, in a gown of flame-coloured brocade, and the young lady of Trinquelage, wearing on her head a great tower of lace puffed and quilled according to the latest fashion of the French court. Farther down the aisle, all dressed in black, with vast pointed wigs and clean-shaven chins, sit Thomas Arnoton the bailiff and Master Ambroy the notary, two sombre spots among these gaudy silks and figured damasks. Then come the fat major-domos, the pages, the outriders, the stewards, and Dame Barbe, with all her keys dangling at her side on a great keyring of fine silver. On the benches in the rear is the lower service—the butlers and maids, the farmers and their families; and last of all, back by the doors, which they half open and discreetly close again, come the cooks to take a little nip of the mass between two sauces, and bring an odour of the Christmas feast into the bedecked church, which is warm with the light of so many tapers.

Can it be the sight of these little white caps that diverts the reverend Father's attention? Is it not rather Garrigou's bell?—that fiendish little bell that tinkles away at the foot of the altar with such infernal haste and seems to say all the time:

'Hurry up! Hurry up! The sooner we've finished, the sooner we shall be at the feast.'

The fact is that every time this devilish little bell peals out, the chaplain forgets his mass, and his mind wanders to the Christmas feast. Visions rise before him of the cooks running busily hither and thither, the ovens glowing like furnaces, warm vapours rising from under half-lifted lids, and through these vapours two mag-nificent turkeys, stuffed, crammed, mottled with truffles . . . Or then again, he sees long files of little pages carrying great dishes wrapped in their tempting fumes, and he is about to enter the dining hall with them for the feast. What ecstasy! Here stands the immense table, laden and dazzling, with peacocks dressed in their fathers, pheasants spreading their bronzed wings, ruby-coloured flagons, pyramids of luscious fruit amid the green foliage, and those wonderful fish that Garrigou spoke of (Garrigou, forsooth!) reclining on a bed of fennel, their pearly scales looking as if they were just from the pond, and a bunch of pungent herbs in their monsterlike nostrils. So vivid is the vision of these marvels that Dom Balaguere actually fancies all these glorious dishes are being served before him, on the very embroideries of the altar-cloth, and two or three times, instead of *Dominus vobiscum* he catches himself saying the *Benedicite*. But except for these slight mistakes the worthy man rattled off the service conscientiously, without skip-ping a line or omitting a genuflection; and all went well to the end of the first mass. For you know, you must know, that on Christmas Eve, the same officiating priest is obliged to say three masses consecutively.

'And that's one!' said the chaplain to himself with a sigh of relief; then, without losing a second, he motioned to his clerk, or him whom he believed to be his clerk, and . . .

Ding-a-ling-ling! Ding-a-ling-ling!
The second mass has begun, and with it Dom Balaguere's sin.

'Quick, quick! let us hurry!' says Garrigou's bell in its shrill, devilish voice, and this time the unfortunate priest, possessed by the demon of gluttony, pounces upon the missal and devours its pages with the avidity of his over-excited appetite. He kneels and rises frantically, barely sketches the sign of the cross and the genuflections, and shortens all his gestures in order to get through sooner. He scarcely extends his arms at the Gospel, or strikes his breast at the *Confiteor*. Between him and the clerk it is hard to tell who mumbles the faster. Verses and responses leap out and jostle each other. The words, half uttered between their teeth—for it would take too long to open their lips every time—die out into unintelligible murmurs.

'*Oremus . . . ps . . . ps . . .*'

'*Mea culpa . . . pa . . . pa . . .*'

Like hurried vintagers crushing the grapes in the vats, they both splashed about in the Latin of the service, spattering it in every direction.

'"*Dom . . . scum!*" says Balaguere.'

'. . . . *Stutuo!*' replies Garrigou; and all the time the accurst little bell jingles in their ears like the sleighbells that are put on stage-horses to make them gallop faster. You may well believe that at such speed a low mass is soon hurried out of the way.

'And that's two,' says the chaplain, all out of breath; then, red in the face, perspiring freely, without taking time to breathe he goes tumbling down the altar steps and . . .

Ding-a-ling-ling! Ding-a-ling-ling!

The third mass has begun. There are only a few steps between him and the dining hall; but alas! as the time approaches, the unfortunate Dom Balaguere's fever of impatience and greediness grows. His imagination waxes more vivid; the fish, the roasted turkeys, are there before him . . . he touches them . . . he—good heavens!—he breathes the perfume of the wines and the savoury fumes of the dishes, and the infernal little bell calls out frantically to him:

'Hurry, hurry! Faster, faster!'

But how on earth can he go faster?—his lips barely move; he no longer pronounces his words—unless, forsooth, he chooses to cheat the good Lord and swindle him out of His mass. And that is just what he does, the wretched man! Yielding to temptation after temptation, he begins by skipping one verse, then two; then he finds the Epistle too long, so he leaves it unfinished; he skims over the Gospel; passes the *Credo* without entering; jumps the *Pater*; salutes the preface from afar; and by leaps and bounds he plunges

25

into eternal damnation, followed by that infamous Garrigou (*Vade retro, Satanas!*), who seconds him with marvellous sympathy, holds up his chasuble, turns the pages two at a time, jostles the lectern, upsets the vases, and constantly rings the little bell faster and louder.

It would be impossible to describe the bewildered expression of the congregation. Compelled to follow, mimicking the priest, through this mass of which they cannot make out a single word, some get up while others kneel, some sit while others stand; and all the phases of this singular service was jumbled together along the benches in confusion of varied postures. The Christmas star on its celestial road, journeying toward the little manger yonder, grows pale at seeing such a frightful confusion.

'The abbé reads too fast; one can't follow him,' murmurs the old dowager marchioness, her voluminous head-dress shaking wildly. Master Arnoton, with his great steel spectacles on his nose, hunts desperately in his prayerbook to find where on earth is the place. But at heart, all these good people, whose minds are equally bent upon the Christmas feast, are not at all disturbed at the idea of following mass at such breakneck speed; and when Dom Balaguere, his face shining, faces them and cries out in a thundering voice, '*Ite, missa est,*' the congregation answers with a '*Deo gratias*' so joyous, so enthusiastic, that one might believe they were already at the table for the first toast of the Christmas feast.

*   *   *

Five minutes later, the assembled lords, with the chaplain in their midst, had taken their seats in the great hall. The castle, brilliantly illumined from top to bottom, echoed with songs and laughter; and the venerable Dom Balaguere planted his fork in a capon's wing, drowning the remorse for his sin in floods of old wine and the savoury juice of meats. He ate and drank so heartily, this poor holy man, that he died in the night of a terrible attack of indigestion, without even having time to repent. By morning he reached heaven, his head still swimming from the odours of the feast; and I leave you to imagine how he was received.

'Get thee gone from my sight, thou wretched Christian!' said the Sovereign Judge, the Master of us all. 'Thy sin is great enough to wipe out the virtues of a lifetime! Ah, thou has stolen from me a midnight mass! Very well, then: thou shalt pay me three hundred masses in its place, and thou shalt not enter into paradise until three hundred Christmas masses have been celebrated in thine own chapel, in the presence of all those who sinned with thee and through thee.'

And this is the true legend of Dom Balaguere, as it is told in the land of the olive tree. The castle of Trinquelage has long ceased to exist; but the chapel stands erect on the crest of Mount Ventoux, in a clump of evergreen oaks. The wind sways its unhinged door, the grass grows over the threshold; there are nests in the angles of the altar and on the sills of the high ogive windows, whose jewelled panes have long ago disappeared. Still, it seems that every year, on Christmas night, a supernatural light wanders among the ruins; and the peasants, on their way to midnight mass and the Christmas feast, see this spectre of a chapel lighted by invisible tapers which burn in the open air, even in the wind and under the snow. You may laugh if you will, but a vine-dresser of the district, named Garrigue, no doubt a descendant of Garrigou, has told me that one one particular Christmas night, being somewhat in liquor, he lost his way on the mountain somewhere near Trinquelage, and this is what he saw. . . . Until 11 o'clock, nothing. Everything was silent and dark. Suddenly, towards midnight, the chimes rang out from the old steeple—old, old chimes that seemed to be ringing ten leagues away. Soon lights began to tremble along the road that climbs to the castle, and vague shadows moved about. Under the portal of the chapel there were faint footsteps, and muffled voices:

'Good evening, Master Arnoton!'

'Good evening, good evening, my children!'

When they had all gone in, the vine-dresser, who was very brave, softly approached, and, looking through the broken door, beheld a singular spectacle. All those shadows that he had seen pass were now seated around the choir in the ruined nave, just as if the old benches were still there. There were fine ladies in brocades and lace head-dresses, gaily bedecked lords, peasants in flowered coats like those our grandfathers wore; all of them old, dusty, faded, weary. Every now and then some night-bird, a habitual lodger in the chapel, awakened by all these lights, would flutter about the tapers, of which the flame rose erect and vague as if it were burning behind a strip of gauze. And what amused Garrigue most was a certain gentleman with great steel spectacles, who constantly shook his huge black wig, on which perched one of those birds, its claws entangled and its wings beating wildly.

A little old man with a childlike figure, knelt in the centre of the choir and frantically shook a tiny bell that had lost its clapper and its voice, while a priest, clad in vestments of old gold, moved hither and thither before the altar repeating orisons of which not a single syllable could be heard.

Without doubt, this was Dom Balaguere in the act of saying his third low mass.

THE COFFIN-MAKER

Alexander Pushkin

The last of the effects of the coffin-maker, Adrian Prokhoroff, were placed upon the hearse, and a couple of sorry-looking jades dragged themselves along for the fourth time from Basmannaia to Nikitskaia, whither the coffin-maker was removing with all his household. After locking up the shop, he posted upon the door a placard announcing that the house was to be let or sold, and then made his way on foot to his new abode. On approaching the little yellow house, which had so long captivated his imagination, and which at last he had bought for a considerable sum, the old coffin-maker was astonished to find that his heart did not rejoice. When he crossed the unfamiliar threshold and found his new home in the greatest confusion, he sighed for his old hovel, where for eighteen years the strictest order had prevailed. He began to scold his two daughters and the servant for their slowness, and then set to work to help them himself. Order was soon established; the ark with the sacred images, the cupboard with the crockery, the table, the sofa, and the bed occupied the corners reserved for them in the back room; in the kitchen and parlour were placed the articles comprising the stock-in-trade of the master—coffins of all colours and of all sizes, together with cupboards containing mourning hats, cloaks and torches.

Over the door was placed a sign representing a fat Cupid with an inverted torch in his hand and bearing this inscription: 'Plain and coloured coffins sold and lined here; coffins also let out on hire, and old ones repaired.'

The girls retired to their bedroom; Adrian made a tour of inspection of his quarters, and then sat down by the window and ordered the tea-urn to be prepared.

The enlightened reader knows that Shakespeare and Walter Scott have both represented their grave-diggers as merry and facetious individuals, in order that the contrast might more forcibly strike our imagination. Out of respect for the truth, we cannot follow their example, and we are compelled to confess that the disposition of our coffin-maker was in perfect harmony with his gloomy occupation. Adrian Prokhoroff was usually gloomy and thoughtful. He rarely opened his mouth, except to scold his daughters when he found them standing idle and gazing out of the window at the passer-by, or to demand for his wares an exorbitant price from those who had the misfortune—and sometimes the good fortune—to need them. Hence it was that Adrian, sitting near the window and drinking his seventh cup of tea, was immersed as usual in melancholy reflections. He thought of the pouring rain which, just a week before, had commenced to beat down during the funeral of the retired brigadier. Many of the cloaks had shrunk in consequence of the downpour, and many of the hats had been put quite out of shape. He foresaw unavoidable expenses, for his old stock of funeral dresses was in a pitiable condition. He hoped to compensate himself for his losses by the burial of old Trukhina, the shopkeeper's wife, who for more than a year had been upon the point of death. But Trukhina lay dying at Rasgouliai, and Prokhoroff was afraid that her heirs, in spite of their promise, would not take the trouble to send so far for him, but would make arrangements with the nearest undertaker.

These reflections were suddenly interrupted by three masonic knocks at the door.

'Who is there?' asked the coffin-maker.

The door opened, and a man, who at the first glance could be recognised as a German artisan, entered the room, and with a jovial air advanced towards the coffin-maker.

'Pardon me, respected neighbour,' said he in that Russian dialect which to this day we cannot hear without a smile: 'Pardon me for disturbing you . . . I wished to make your acquaintance as soon as possible. I am a shoemaker, my name is Gottlieb Schultz, and I live across the street, in that little house just facing your windows. Tomorrow I am going to celebrate my silver wedding, and I have come to invite you and your daughters to dine with us.'

The invitation was cordially accepted. The coffin-maker asked the shoemaker to seat himself and take a cup of tea, and thanks to the open-hearted disposition of Gottlieb Schultz, they were soon engaged in friendly conversation.

'How is business with you?' asked Adrian.

'Just so so,' replied Schultz; 'I cannot complain. My wares are not like yours: the living can do without shoes, but the dead cannot do without coffins.'

'Very true,' observed Adrian; 'but if a living person hasn't anything to buy shoes with, you cannot find fault with him, he goes about barefooted; but a dead beggar gets his coffin for nothing.'

In this manner the conversation was carried on between them for some time; at last the shoemaker rose and took leave of the coffin-maker, renewing his invitation.

The next day, exactly at twelve o'clock, the coffin-maker and his daughters issued from the doorway of their newly-purchased residence, and directed their steps towards the abode of their neighbour. I will not stop to describe the Russian *caftan* of Adrian Prokhoroff, nor the European toilettes of Akoulina and Daria, deviating in this respect from the usual custom of modern novelists. But I do not think it superfluous to observe that they both had on the yellow cloaks and red shoes, which they were accustomed to don on solemn occasions only.

The shoemaker's little dwelling was filled with guests, consisting chiefly of German artisans with their wives and foremen. Of the Russian officials there was present but one, Yourko the Finn, a watchman, who, in spite of his humble calling, was the special object of the host's attention. For twenty-five years he had faithfully discharged the duties of postilion of Pogorelsky. The conflagration of 1812, which destroyed the ancient capital, destroyed also his little yellow watch-house. But immediately after the expulsion of the enemy, a new one appeared in its place, painted grey and with white Doric columns, and Yourko began again to pace to and fro before it, with his axe and grey coat of mail. He was known to the greater part of the Germans who lived near the Nikitskaia Gate, and some of them had even spent the night from Sunday to Monday beneath his roof.

Adrian immediately made himself acquainted with him, as with a man whom, sooner or later, he might have need of, and when the guests took their places at the table, they sat down beside each other. Herr Schultz and his wife, and their daughter Lotchen, a young girl of seventeen, did the honours of the table and helped the cook to serve. The beer flowed in streams; Yourko ate like four, and Adrian in no way yielded to him; his daughters, however, stood upon their dignity. The conversation, which was carried on in German, gradually grew more and more boisterous. Suddenly the host requested a moment's attention, and uncorking a sealed bottle, he said with a loud voice in Russian:

'To the health of my good Louise!'

The champagne foamed. The host tenderly kissed the fresh face of his partner, and the guests drank noisily to the health of the good Louise.

'To the health of my amiable guests!' exclaimed the host, uncorking a second bottle; and the guests thanked him by draining their glasses once more.

Then followed a succession of toasts. The health of each individual guest was drunk; they drank to the health of Moscow and to quite a dozen little German towns; they drank to the health of all corporations in general and of each in particular; they drank to the health of the masters and foremen. Adrian drank with enthusiasm and became so merry, that he proposed a facetious toast to himself. Suddenly one of the guests, a fat baker, raised his glass and exclaimed:

'To the health of those for whom we work, our customers!'

This proposal, like all the others, was joyously and unanimously received. The guests began to salute each other; the tailor bowed to the shoemaker, the shoemaker to the tailor, the baker to both, the whole company to the baker, and so on. In the midst of these mutual congratulations, Yourko exclaimed, turning to his neighbour:

'Come, little father! Drink to the health of your corpses!'

Everybody laughed, but the coffin-maker considered himself insulted, and frowned. Nobody noticed it, the guests continued to drink, and the bell had already rung for vespers when they rose from the table.

The guests dispersed at a late hour, the greater part of them in a very merry mood. The fat baker and the bookbinder, whose face seemed as if bound in red morocco, linked their arms in those of Yourko and conducted him back to his little watch-house, thus observing the proverb: 'One good turn deserves another.'

The coffin-maker returned home drunk and angry.

'Why is it,' he exclaimed aloud, 'why is it that my trade is not as honest as any other? Is a coffin-maker brother to the hangman? Why did those heathens laugh? Is a coffin-maker a buffoon? I wanted to invite them to my new dwelling and give them a feast, but now I'll do nothing of the kind. Instead of inviting them, I will invite those for whom I work: the orthodox dead.'

'What is the matter, little father?' said the servant, who was engaged at that moment in taking off his boots: 'why do you talk such nonsense? Make the sign of the cross! Invite the dead to your new house! What folly!'

'Yes, by the Lord! I will invite them,' continued Adrian, 'and that, too, for tomorrow! . . . Do me the favour, my benefactors, to come and feast with me tomorrow evening; I will regale you with what God has sent me.'

With these words the coffin-maker turned into bed and soon began to snore.

It was still dark when Adrian was awakened out of his sleep. Trukhina, the shopkeeper's wife, had died during the course of that very night, and a special messenger was sent off on horseback by her bailiff to carry the news to Adrian. The coffin-maker gave him ten copecks to buy brandy with, dressed himself as hastily as possible, took a *droshky* and set out for Rasgouliai. Before the door of the house in which the deceased lay, the police had already taken their stand, and the trades-people were passing backwards and forwards, like ravens that smell a dead body. The deceased lay upon a table, yellow as wax, but not yet disfigured by decomposition. Around her stood her relatives, neighbours and domestic servants. All the windows were open; tapers were burning; and the priests were reading the prayers for the dead. Adrian went up to the nephew of Trukhina, a young shopman in a fashionable surtout, and informed him that the coffin, wax candles, pall, and the other funeral accessories would be immediately delivered with all possible exactitude. The heir thanked him in an absent-minded manner, saying that he would not bargain about the price, but would rely upon him acting in everything according to his conscience. The coffin-maker, in accordance with his usual custom, vowed that he would not charge him too much, exchanged significant glances with the bailiff, and then departed to commence operations.

The whole day was spent in passing to and fro between Rasgouliai and the Nikitskaia Gate. Towards evening everything was finished, and he returned home on foot, after having dismissed his driver. It was a moonlight night. The coffin-maker reached the Nikitskaia Gate in safety. Near the Church of the Ascension he was hailed by our acquaintance Yourko, who, recognising the coffin-maker reached the Nikitskaia Gate in safety. Near the Church of the Ascension he was hailed by our acquaintance Yourko, who, recognising the coffin-maker, wished him goodnight. It was late. The coffin-maker was just approaching his house, when suddenly he fancied he saw some one approach his gate, open the wicket, and disappear within.

'What does that mean?' thought Adrian. 'Who can be wanting me again? Can it be a thief come to rob me? Or have my foolish girls got lovers coming after them? It means no good, I fear!'

And the coffin-maker thought of calling his friend Yourko to his assistance. But at that moment, another person approached the wicket and was about to enter, but seeing the master of the house hastening towards him, he stopped and took off his three-cornered hat. His face seemed familiar to Adrian, but in his hurry he had not been able to examine it closely.

'You are favouring me with a visit,' said Adrian, out of breath. 'Walk in, I beg of you.'

'Don't stand on ceremony, little father,' replied the other, in a hollow voice; 'you go first, and show your guests the way.'

Adrian had no time to spend upon ceremony. The wicket was open; he ascended the steps followed by the other. Adrian thought he could hear people walking about in his rooms.

'What the devil does all this mean!' he thought to himself, and he hastened to enter. But the sight that met his eyes caused his legs to give way beneath him.

The room was full of corpses. The moon, shining through the windows, lit up their yellow and blue faces, sunken mouths, dim, half-closed eyes, and protruding noses. Adrian, with horror, recognised in them people that he himself had buried, and in the guest who entered with him, the brigadier who had been buried during the pouring rain. They all, men and women, surrounded the coffin-maker, with bowings and salutations, except one poor fellow lately buried gratis, who, conscious and ashamed of his rags, did not venture to approach, but meekly kept aloof in a corner. All the others were decently dressed: the female corpses in caps and ribbons, the officials in uniforms, but with their beards unshaven, the tradesmen in their holiday *caftans*.

'You see, Prokhoroff,' said the brigadier in the name of all the honourable company, 'we have all risen in response to your invitation. Only those have stopped at home who were unable to come, who have crumbled to pieces and have nothing left but fleshless bones. But even of these there was one who hadn't the patience to remain behind—so much did he want to come and see you . . .'

At this moment a little skeleton pushed his way through the crowd and approached Adrian. His fleshless face smiled affably at the coffin-maker. Shreds of green and red cloth and rotten linen hung on him here and there as on a pole, and the bones of his feet rattled inside his big jackboots, like pestles in mortars.

'You do not recognise me, Prokhoroff,' said the skeleton. 'Don't you remember the retired sergeant of the Guards, Peter Petrovitch Kourilkin, the same to whom, in the year 1799, you sold your first coffin, and that, too, of deal instead of oak?'

With these words the corpse stretched out his bony arms towards him; but Adrian, collecting all his strength, shrieked and pushed him from him. Peter Petrovitch staggered, fell, and crumbled all to pieces. Among the corpses arose a murmur of indignation; all stood up for the honour of their companion, and they overwhelmed Adrian with such threats and imprecations, that the poor host, deafened by their shrieks and almost crushed to death, lost his presence of mind, fell upon the bones of the retired sergeant of the Guards, and swooned away.

For some time the sun had been shining upon the bed on which lay the coffin-maker. At last he opened his eyes and saw before him the servant attending to the tea-urn. With horror, Adrian recalled all the incidents of the previous day. Trukhina, the brigadier, and the sergeant, Kourilkin, rose vaguely before his imagination. He waited in silence for the servant to open the conversation and inform him of the events of the night.

'How you have slept, little father Adrian Prokhorovitch!' said Aksinia, handing him his dressing-gown. 'Your neighbour, the tailor, has been here, and the watchman also called to inform you that today is his name-day; but you were so sound asleep, that we did not wish to wake you.'

'Did anyone come for me from the late Trukhina?'

'The late? Is she dead, then?'

'What a fool you are! Didn't you yourself help me yesterday to prepare the things for her funeral?'

'Have you taken leave of your senses, little father, or have you not yet recovered from the effects of yesterday's drinking-bout? What funeral was there yesterday? You spent the whole day feasting at the German's, and then came home drunk and threw yourself upon the bed, and have slept till this hour, when the bells have already rung for mass.'

'Really!' said the coffin-maker, greatly relieved.

'Yes, indeed,' replied the servant.

'Well, since that is the case, make the tea as quickly as possible and call my daughters.'

LOST HEARTS

M.R. James

*   *   *

It was, as far as I can ascertain, in September of the
year 1811 that a postchaise drew up before the door
of Aswarby Hall, in the heart of Lincolnshire. The
little boy who was the only passenger in the chaise,
and who jumped out as soon as it had stopped,
looked about him with the keenest curiosity during
the short interval that elapsed between the ringing of
the bell and the opening of the hall door. He saw a
tall, square, red-brick house, built in the reign of
Anne ; a stone-pillared porch had been added in the

purer classical style of 1790; the windows of the house were many, tall and narrow, with small panes and thick white woodwork. A pediment, pierced with a round window, crowned the front. There were wings to right and left, connected by curious glazed galleries, supported by colonnades, with the central block. These wings plainly contained the stables and offices of the house. Each was surmounted by an ornamental cupola with a gilded vane.

An evening light shone on the building, making the window-panes glow like so many fires. Away from the Hall in front stretched a flat park studded with oaks and fringed with firs, which stood out against the sky. The clock in the church-tower, buried in trees on the edge of the park, only its golden weather-cock catching the light, was striking six, and the sound came gently beating down the wind. It was altogether a pleasant impression, though tinged with the sort of melancholy appropriate to an evening in early autumn, that was conveyed to the mind of the boy who was standing in the porch waiting for the door to open to him.

He had just come from Warwickshire, and some six months ago had been left an orphan. Now, owing to the generous and unexpected offer of his elderly cousin, Mr. Abney, he had come to live at Aswarby. The offer was unexpected, because all who knew anything of Mr. Abney looked upon him as a somewhat austere recluse, into whose steady-going household the advent of a small boy would import a new and, it seemed, incongruous element. The truth is that very little was known of Mr. Abney's pursuits or temper. The Professor of Greek at Cambridge had been heard to say that no one knew more of the religious beliefs of the later pagans than did the owner of Aswarby. Certainly his library contained all the then available books bearing on the Mysteries, the Orphic poems, the worship of Mithras, and the Neo-Platonists. In the marble-paved hall stood a fine group of Mithras slaying a bull, which had been imported from the Levant at great expense by the owner. He had contributed a description of it to the *Gentleman's Magazine*, and he had written a remarkable series of articles in the *Critical Museum* on the superstitions of the Romans of the Lower Empire. He was looked upon, in fine, as a man wrapped up in his books, and it was a matter of great surprise among his neighbours that he should ever have heard of his orphan cousin, Stephen Elliott, much more that he should have volunteered to make him an inmate of Aswarby Hall.

Whatever may have been expected by his neighbours, it is certain that Mr. Abney – the tall, the thin, the austere – seemed inclined to give his young cousin a kindly reception. The moment the front-door was opened he darted out of his study, rubbing his hands with delight.

'How are you, my boy? – how are you? How old are you?' said he – 'that is, you are not too much tired, I hope, by your journey to eat your supper?'.

'No, thank you, sir,' said Master Elliott; 'I am pretty well.'

'That's a good lad,' said Mr. Abney. 'And how old are you, my boy?'

It seemed a little odd that he should have asked the question twice in the first two minutes of their acquaintance.

'I'm twelve years old next birthday, sir,' said Stephen.

'And when is your birthday, my dear boy? Eleventh of September, eh? That's well – that's very well. Nearly a year hence, isn't it? I like – ha, ha! – I like to get these things down in my book. Sure it's twelve? Certain?'

'Yes, quite sure, sir.'

'Well, well! Take him to Mrs. Bunch's room, Parkes, and let him have his tea – supper – whatever it is.'

'Yes, sir,' answered the staid Mr. Parkes; and conducted Stephen to the lower regions.

Mrs. Bunch was the most comfortable and human person whom Stephen had as yet met in Aswarby. She made him completely at home; they were great friends in a quarter of an hour: and great friends they remained. Mrs. Bunch had been born in the neighbourhood some fifty-five years before the date of Stephen's arrival, and her residence at the Hall was of twenty years' standing. Consequently, if anyone knew the ins and outs of the house and the district, Mrs. Bunch knew them; and she was by no means disinclined to communicate her information.

Certainly there were plenty of things about the Hall and the Hall gardens which Stephen, who was of an adventurous and inquiring turn, was anxious to have explained to him. 'Who built the temple at the end of the laurel walk? Who was the old man whose picture hung on the staircase, sitting at a table, with a skull under his hand?' These and many similar points were cleared up by the resources of Mrs. Bunch's powerful intellect. There were others, however, of which the explanations furnished were less satisfactory.

One November evening Stephen was sitting by the fire in the housekeeper's room reflecting on his surroundings.

'Is Mr. Abney a good man, and will he go to heaven?' he suddenly asked, with the peculiar confidence which children possess in the ability of their elders to settle these questions, the decision of which is believed to be reserved for other tribunals.

'Good? – bless the child!' said Mrs. Bunch. 'Master's as kind a soul as ever I see! Didn't I never tell you of the little boy as he took in out of the street, as you may say, this seven years back? And the little girl, two years after I first come here?'

'No. Do tell me all about them, Mrs. Bunch – now this minute!'

'Well,' said Mrs. Bunch, 'the little girl I don't seem to recollect so much about. I know master brought her back with him from his walk one day, and give orders to Mrs. Ellis, as was housekeeper then, as she should be took every care with. And the pore child hadn't no one belonging to her – she told me so her own self – and here she lived with us a matter of three weeks it might be; and then, whether she were somethink of a gipsy in her blood or what not, but one morning she out of her bed afore any of us had opened a eye, and neither track nor yet trace of her have I set eyes on since. Master was wonderful put about, and had all the ponds dragged; but it's my belief she was had away by them gipsies, for there was singing round the house for as much as an hour the night she went, and Parkes, he declare as he heard them a-calling in the woods all that afternoon. Dear, dear! An odd child she was, so silent in her ways and all, but I was wonderful taken up with her, so domesticated she was – surprising.'

'And what about the little boy?' said Stephen.

'Ah, that pore boy!' sighed Mrs. Bunch. 'He were a foreigner – Jevanny he called hisself – and he come a-tweaking his 'urdy-gurdy round and about the drive one winter day, and master 'ad him in that minute, and ast all about where he came from, and how old he was, and how he made his way, and where was his relatives, and all as kind as heart could wish. But it went the same way with him. They're a hunruly lot, them foreign nations, I do suppose, and he was off one fine morning just the same as the girl. Why he went and what he done was our question for as much as a year after; for he never took his 'urdy-gurdy, and there it lays on the shelf.'

The remainder of the evening was spent by Stephen in miscellaneous cross-examination of Mrs. Bunch and in efforts to extract a tune from the hurdy-gurdy.

That night he had a curious dream. At the end of the passage at the top of the house, in which his bedroom was situated, there was an old disused bathroom. It was kept locked, but the upper half of the door was glazed, and, since the muslin curtains which used to hang there had long been gone, you could look in and see the lead-lined bath affixed to the wall on the right hand, with its head towards the window.

On the night of which I am speaking, Stephen Elliott found himself, as he thought, looking through the glazed door. The moon was shining through the window, and he was gazing at a figure which lay in the bath.

His description of what he saw reminds me of what I once beheld myself in the famous vaults of St. Michan's Church in Dublin, which possess the horrid property of preserving corpses from decay for centuries. A figure inexpressibly thin and pathetic, of a dusty leaden colour, enveloped in a shroud-like garment, the thin lips crooked into a faint and dreadful smile, the hands pressed tightly over the region of the heart.

As he looked upon it, a distant, almost inaudible moan seemed to issue from its lips, and the arms began to stir. The terror of the sight forced Stephen backwards, and he awoke to the fact that he was indeed standing on the cold boarded floor of the passage in the full light of the moon. With a courage which I do not think can be common among boys of his age, he went to the door of the bathroom to ascertain if the figure of his dream were really there. It was not, and he went back to bed.

Mrs. Bunch was much impressed next morning by his story, and went so far as to replace the muslin curtain over the glazed door of the bathroom. Mr. Abney, moreover, to whom he confided his experiences at breakfast, was greatly interested, and made notes of the matter in what he called 'his book.'

The spring equinox was approaching, as Mr. Abney frequently reminded his cousin, adding that this had been always considered by the ancients to be a critical time for the young: that Stephen would do well to take care of himself, and to shut his bedroom window at night; and that Censorinus had some valuable remarks on the subject. Two incidents that occurred about this time made an impression upon Stephen's mind.

The first was after an unusually uneasy and oppressed night that he had passed – though he could not recall any particular dream that he had had.

The following evening Mrs. Bunch was occupying herself in mending his nightgown.

'Gracious me, Master Stephen!' she broke forth rather irritably, 'how do you manage to tear your nightdress all to flinders this way? Look here, sir, what trouble you do give to poor servants that have to darn and mend after you!'

There was indeed a most destructive and apparently wanton series of slits or scorings in the garment, which would undoubtedly require a skilful needle to make good. They were confined to the left side of the chest – long, parallel slits, about six inches in length, some of them not quite piercing the texture of the linen. Stephen could only express his entire ignorance of their origin: he was sure they were not there the night before.

'But,' he said, 'Mrs. Bunch, they are just the same as the scratches on the outside of my bedroom door; and I'm sure I never had anything to do with making *them*.'

Mrs. Bunch gazed at him open-mouthed, then snatched up a candle, departed hastily from the room, and was heard making her way upstairs. In a few minutes she came down.

'Well,' she said, 'Master Stephen, it's a funny thing to me how them marks and scratches can 'a' come there – too high up for any cat or dog to 'ave made 'em, much less a rat: for all the world like a China-man's fingernails, as my uncle in the tea-trade used to tell us of when we was girls together. I wouldn't say nothing to master, not if I was you, Master Stephen, my dear; and just turn the key of the door when you go to your bed.'

'I always do, Mrs. Bunch, as soon as I've said my prayers.'

'Ah, that's a good child: always say your prayers, and then no one can't hurt you.'

Herewith Mrs. Bunch addressed herself to mending the injured nightgown, with intervals of meditation, until bed-time. This was on a Friday night in March, 1812.

43

On the following evening the usual duet of Stephen and Mrs. Bunch was augmented by the sudden arrival of Mr. Parkes, the butler, who as a rule kept himself rather *to* himself in his own pantry. He did not see that Stephen was there: he was, moreover, flustered and less slow of speech than was his wont.

'Master may get up his own wine, if he likes, of an evening,' was his first remark. 'Either I do it in the daytime or not at all, Mrs. Bunch. I don't know what it may be: very like it's the rats, or the wind got into the cellars; but I'm not so young as I was, and I can't go through with it as I have done.'

'Well, Mr. Parkes, you know it is a surprising place for the rats, is the Hall.'

'I'm not denying that, Mrs. Bunch; and, to be sure, many a time I've heard the tale from the men in the shipyards about the rat that could speak. I never laid no confidence in that before; but to-night, if I'd demeaned myself to lay my ear to the door of the further bin, I could pretty much have heard what they was saying.'

'Oh, there, Mr. Parkes, I've no patience with your fancies! Rats talking in the wine-cellar indeed!'

'Well, Mrs. Bunch, I've no wish to argue with you: all I say is, if you choose to go to the far bin, and lay your ear to the door, you may prove my words this minute.'

'What nonsense you do talk, Mr. Parkes – not fit for children to listen to! Why, you'll be frightening Master Stephen there out of his wits.'

'What! Master Stephen?' said Parkes, awaking to

the consciousness of the boy's presence. 'Master Stephen knows well enough when I'm a-playing a joke with you, Mrs. Bunch.'

In fact, Master Stephen knew much too well to suppose that Mr. Parkes had in the first instance intended a joke. He was interested, not altogether pleasantly, in the situation; but all his questions were unsuccessful in inducing the butler to give any more detailed account of his experiences in the wine-cellar.

We have now arrived at March 24, 1812. It was a day of curious experiences for Stephen: a windy, noisy day, which filled the house and the gardens with a restless impression. As Stephen stood by the fence of the grounds, and looked out into the park, he felt as if an endless procession of unseen people were sweeping past him on the wind, borne on resistlessly and aimlessly, vainly striving to stop themselves, to catch at something that might arrest their flight and bring them once again into contact with the living world of which they had formed a part. After luncheon that day Mr. Abney said:

'Stephen, my boy, do you think you could manage to come to me to-night as late as eleven o'clock in my study? I shall be busy until that time, and I wish to show you something connected with your future life which it is most important that you should know. You are not to mention this matter to Mrs. Bunch nor to anyone else in the house; and you had better go to your room at the usual time.'

Here was a new excitement added to life: Stephen eagerly grasped at the opportunity of sitting up till eleven o'clock. He looked in at the library door on his way upstairs that evening, and saw a brazier, which he had often noticed in the corner of the room, moved out before the fire; an old silver-gilt cup stood on the table, filled with red wine, and some written sheets of paper lay near it. Mr. Abney was sprinkling some incense on the brazier from a round silver box as Stephen passed, but did not seem to notice his step.

The wind had fallen, and there was a still night and a full moon. At about ten o'clock Stephen was standing at the open window of his bedroom, looking out over the country. Still as the night was, the mysterious population of the distant moonlit woods was not yet lulled to rest. From time to time strange cries as of lost and despairing wanderers sounded from across the mere. They might be the notes of owls or water-birds, yet they did not quite resemble either sound. Were not they coming nearer? Now they sounded from the nearer side of the water, and in a few moments they seemed to be floating about among the shrubberies. Then they ceased; but just as Stephen was thinking of shutting the window and resuming his reading of 'Robinson Crusoe,' he caught sight of two figures standing on the gravelled terrace that ran along the garden side of the Hall – the figures of a boy and girl, as it seemed; they stood side by side, looking up at the windows. Something in the form of the girl recalled irresistibly his dream of the figure in the bath. The boy inspired him with more acute fear.

Whilst the girl stood still, half smiling, with her hands clasped over her heart, the boy, a thin shape, with black hair and ragged clothing, raised his arms in the air with an appearance of menace and of unappeasable hunger and longing. The moon shone upon his almost transparent hands, and Stephen saw that the nails were fearfully long and that the light shone through them. As he stood with his arms thus raised, he disclosed a terrifying spectacle. On the left side of his chest there opened a black and gaping rent; and there fell upon Stephen's brain, rather than upon his ear, the impression of one of those hungry and desolate cries that he had heard resounding over the woods of Aswarby all that evening. In another moment this dreadful pair had moved swiftly and noiselessly over the dry gravel, and he saw them no more.

Inexpressibly frightened as he was, he determined to take his candle and go down to Mr. Abney's study, for the hour appointed for their meeting was near at hand. The study or library opened out of the front-hall on one side, and Stephen, urged on by his terrors, did not take long in getting there. To effect an entrance was not so easy. It was not locked, he felt sure, for the key was on the outside of the door as usual. His repeated knocks produced no answer. Mr. Abney was engaged: he was speaking. What! why did he try to cry out? and why was the cry choked in his throat? Had he, too, seen the mysterious children?

But now everything was quiet, and the door yielded to Stephen's terrified and frantic pushing.

On the table in Mr. Abney's study certain papers were found which explained the situation to Stephen Elliott when he was of an age to understand them. The most important sentences were as follows:

'It was a belief very strongly and generally held by the ancients – of whose wisdom in these matters I have had such experience as induces me to place confidence in their assertions – that by enacting certain processes, which to us moderns have something of a barbaric complexion, a very remarkable enlightenment of the spiritual faculties in man may be attained: that, for example, by absorbing the personalities of a certain number of his fellow-creatures, an individual may gain a complete ascendancy over those orders of spiritual beings which control the elemental forces of our universe.

'It is recorded of Simon Magus that he was able to fly in the air, to become invisible, or to assume any form he pleased, by the agency of the soul of a boy whom, to use the libellous phrase employed by the author of the "Clementine Recognitions," he had "murdered." I find it set-down, moreover, with considerable detail in the writings of Hermes Trismegistus, that similar happy results may be produced by the absorptions of the hearts of not less than three human beings below the age of twenty-one years. To the testing of the truth of this receipt I have devoted the greater part of the last twenty years, selecting as the *corpora vilia* of my experiment such persons as could conveniently be removed without occasioning a sensible gap in society. The first step I effected by the removal of óne Phœbe Stanley, a girl of gipsy extraction, on March 24, 1792. The second, by the removal of a wandering Italian lad, named Giovanni Paoli, on the night of March 23, 1805. The final "victim" – to employ a word repugnant in the highest degree to my feelings – must be my cousin, Stephen Elliott. His day must be this March 24, 1812.

'The best means of effecting the required absorption is to remove the heart from the *living* subject, to reduce it to ashes, and to mingle them with about a pint of some red wine, preferably port. The remains of the first two subjects, at least, it will be well to conceal: a disused bath-room or wine-cellar will be found convenient for such a purpose. Some annoyance may be experienced from the psychic portion of the subjects, which popular language dignifies with the name of ghosts. But the man of philosophic temperament – to whom alone the experiment is appropriate – will be little prone to attach importance to the feeble efforts of these beings to wreak their vengeance on him. I contemplate with the liveliest satisfaction the enlarged and emancipated existence which the experiment, if successful, will confer on me; not only placing me beyond the reach of human justice (so-called), but eliminating to a great extent the prospect of death itself.'

Mr. Abney was found in his chair, his head thrown back, his face stamped with an expression of rage, fright, and mortal pain. In his left side was a terrible lacerated wound, exposing the heart. There was no blood on his hands, and a long knife that lay on the table was perfectly clean. A savage wild-cat might have inflicted the injuries. The window of the study was open, and it was the opinion of the coroner that Mr. Abney had met his death by the agency of some wild creature. But Stephen Elliott's study of the papers I have quoted led him to a very different conclusion.

* * *

Sweeney Todd, The Demon Barber

Thomas Prest

I

Near Temple Bar, at the end of Fleet Street, there stood, in the days of George II, a barber's establishment which was conducted by a man named Sweeney Todd. Its outward appearance would compare very unfavourably with any similar institution of the present day, which may also be said of most other businesses of that period, for shopkeepers merely hung out their signs and made little or no pretence of displaying their wares.

But Sweeney Todd's shop presented a mean, dirty, repulsive appearance, for in keeping with the custom of his profession he practised the minor arts of surgery, such as bleeding, and pulling out teeth; so, in addition to the parti-coloured pole projecting from the door, there was at the lower part of the window a row of porringers of pewter and blue and white delf, filled with coagulated blood; while some of the upper panes were adorned with a fanciful arrangement of rotten teeth; and as he united to his vocation the art of dressing and renovating wigs, he added the sign of a grizzly old peruke stuck on a wooden featureless block.

The unpleasant aspect of the exterior was well borne out by the dinginess that prevailed inside, where all the paraphernalia hinted at in the window was to be found in the frowsiest profusion.

At a bench within the shop stood Sweeney Todd dressing a wig, with his apprentice close at hand, timidly watching his movements. He was not a pleasant-looking man, this barber; his brows were low and sullen, his cheekbones high, his nose short and pugnacious, and his hard mouth and square jaw suggested brutal selfishness, which was encouraged by his powerful physique.

'Tobias Wragg,' growled Sweeney, without shifting his eyes from his work, 'you're a lucky dog! Don't you think you're a lucky dog to be here learning an honourable and lucrative profession under such a kind and respected master as myself? Eh?' A pause. 'Haven't you got a tongue?' Sweeney turned and scowled.

'Y'yes, sir,' trembled the boy, painfully uncertain as to what his master expected of him.

'Listen to me seriously, Tobias,' said Sweeney with emphasis, 'you are now my apprentice, bound to me body and soul until you are twenty-one. If you attend to business and merit my approval you may have a comfortable and profitable time with me – I shall not tell you what I expect from you, but I shall watch you, and if you turn out the sort of lad I hope, you will have nothing to complain of, and you may be a rich man some day; but, understand this, if you don't do what I require, if you go against me in any way, if you notice things that are not intended for you to notice, or if you talk outside of anything that takes place here, I'll slit your throat as sure as you are alive. Do you hear, you lout?'

The poor boy, greatly alarmed, was about to give an assurance that he would always do his best to please, when the door was opened and a young man attired in nautical style, and bearing on his good-looking face the bronze of tropical skies, entered the shop. This was Mark Ingestre, whose fate closely concerns this story. Sweeney turned from his work and scrutinised his visitor whilst awaiting his commands.

'Good day to you, Mr Barber, may I trouble you to shave me?' said he.

'Why, of course, you may,' answered Sweeney, 'and I venture to remark that I have rarely shaved a face so gloriously tanned as yours. I presume you have been sailing under sunny skies?'

'Yes, I have known what a hot sun is; but I went to the East for a purpose, determined not to return until it was accomplished. And now I am back again in dear old London with my first great object achieved, and the rest soon will be. But I am in haste to visit my dearest friend, and perhaps you can assist me. I find that Mr Oakley, the spectacle maker, has left Fleet Street – do you know his present address?'

'I do, sir,' replied Sweeney. 'He now lives in Fore Street, and outside you will see the big pair of spectacles that adorned his shop in Fleet Street. Sit down, sir – this chair, please.'

Sweeney always tried to learn as much as possible concerning his patrons, so while he prepared to commence operations he remarked that he had heard much of the wealth of the Indies, but those he knew who had been there had but little to show for their toil. He hoped his visitor had fared better.

'I admit that for a long time I had no luck,' said Mark, 'but when a man can show a packet like this he has little to complain of.' As he spoke he produced a beautifully wrought gold casket. Sweeney was all attention.

'That's wonderfully fine,' he said.

'But not so fine as the contents. Look!' said Mark, opening the box and displaying some magnificent pearls. Sweeney's little eyes glittered.

'I don't know anything about pearls, but they look grand. I shouldn't think you'd take less than a hundred pounds for them.'

'A hundred pounds!' laughed Mark, 'why they are worth £12,000.'

'Really! Well, I'm proud of the honour of shaving you,' said the barber. 'Tobias, go to Mr Crick, in Butcher Row, and ask him if he can oblige me with change for a guinea.'

'I can accommodate you with that,' remarked Mark, putting his hand into his pocket.

'Many thanks,' smiled Todd, 'but it is not so much the change I require as a little outstanding matter which I hope the appearance of my apprentice may bring to his mind.'

He followed Tobias to the door as if to give him further instructions, but his object was to put on the catch. Then, having rapidly lathered Mark's chin, he took a few deliberate steps towards a large cupboard, which he opened, and keeping his eyes on his visitor, who lay with his head back waiting for the shaving to commence, Todd inserted his arm and grasped a lever: there followed a swift, soft, churning sound, the floor opened, and the chair with its burden disappeared. In a few seconds *the chair rose empty*.

Sweeney closed the cupboard, scattered sawdust where it had been disturbed, and picked up the casket. 'Just as well that didn't go with him,' he muttered, as he raised the catch on the door, 'although I shall have to see what else he has got shortly. It is well I waited for this, although I am rich enough without it, and prudence prompts me to get away before my greed of gold proves my undoing.'

Tobias returned at this moment, and so quietly that he startled Sweeney, who hastily thrusting the casket under his apron, turned furiously upon his unfortunate apprentice demanding to know what he meant by creeping back like a spy. He answered that he was afraid of disturbing him in the act of shaving somebody. Unfortunately he saw Mark's hat and stick, and thoughtlessly called Sweeney's attention to them, which infuriated him beyond measure, and he was about to rush at the boy when a negro's head appeared in the doorway.

'Well, Satan, what do you want?' roared Todd.

'Massa Ingestre, where he be?'

'How should I know where he is? Who is he?'

'He came here for shave. I wait for him outside.'

'Well, he's gone, and you go after him.'

'He not gone. I wait outside all time.'

It took Sweeney all his time to get rid of the black, and he was much rattled about it, for he felt there was danger in store for him. Many remarks had been made about mysterious disappearances during the past few months, and many enquiries had been made at his shop by friends of the missing ones, who were stated to have set out intending to call at the barber's, and in consequence he was greatly agitated, for he felt that Tobias had only to mention the hat, stick, and casket, to provide a rope for his neck.

'Yes,' he muttered, 'I'll get away as soon as I can, without a word to anyone.'

But avarice held him in a grip, and while he planned a disappearance he was considering how to dispose of the pearls. Sounds of a brawl in the street reached him, but he was too depressed to seek the reason. The door opened, and amid jeers and shouts, a gentleman entered the shop. Sweeney could hardly believe his eyes – here was the very man to help him out of his first perplexity, Mr Parmine, the eminent goldsmith and jeweller.

'Good evening, Mr Todd,' he said, 'I have been molested

unfortunately in the street just now, my hat was knocked off and my wig snatched, but although I recovered it there is too much mud on it for comfort, so please do your best to set it right.'

Sweeney was thinking hard. He realised that Tobias was in the way. 'Tobias, you can go home, and see that you are early in the morning.' He followed Tobias to the door, and quietly released the catch.

While he endeavoured to restore the outraged glory of the wig Todd spoke casually about precious stones in order that he might lead to the sale of the pearls. Mr Parmine remarked that precious stones were in no demand, the only things asked for being pearls.

'I have some pearls that I might dispose of,' said Sweeney; 'would you care to buy them?'

'Where are they?' asked Mr Parmine.

'Here,' and Sweeney handed him the casket looking keenly at his face to read his thoughts. Mr Parmine was a jeweller of experience, but with all his self-control he did not entirely conceal his surprise.

'H'm. They look well, don't they? Wonderful how cleverly they get up these imitations! The box is not bad either. What do you think of £50 for the lot?'

'I would rather not tell you what I think,' said Sweeney, striving to keep his temper. 'Hand them over!'

'Well, now I come to look at them a little closer, I think, perhaps, I might be able to manage a little more. Shall we say £100?'

'No,' said Todd savagely. 'I know what their value is and so do you.'

'What do you think they are worth then?'

'Twelve thousand pounds, and I am willing to sell them to you so that you can make a substantial profit, but I want no nonsense or haggling.'

'Well, if they are genuine – I didn't think they were – I daresay I can find a purchaser for £11,000; if so I will advance £8,000.'

'That will satisfy me. I will call tomorrow morning for the money.'

'I am afraid I shall not be able to let you have it – there are important matters to be considered first. A string of valuable pearls cannot be bought like common trinkets; the vendor must give every satisfaction as to how he came by them.'

'And who, may I enquire, will question a man of your standing in the trade?' asked Sweeney, trying to be calm.

'That is not the point; if I give you a large sum for an article I am entitled to know how it came into your possession as a safeguard against possible future complications.'

'That is to say that you don't care how I came to possess the property provided I sell it to you at a thief's price, but if I want its real value you mean to be particular.'

'For a man in your position to possess a £12,000 string of pearls requires explanation and I insist that it is given before a magistrate. Come!'

Mr Parmine, casket in hand, turned towards the door, but as he did so Sweeney sprang upon him with the howl of a fiend. The suddenness of the attack, and the blind fury with which it was delivered, gave him an advantage, and he forced the jeweller towards the fatal chair, intending to strangle him in it, for he could not hold him there and manipulate the lever; but scarcely had he thrown him in the chair than the trap-door opened without assistance, and Sweeney was only just able to save himself from disappearing with his victim.

Sweeney was terribly alarmed at his narrow escape, and his blood ran cold when he contemplated the failure of his trap. He kicked the casket on the floor and cursed it. What was he to do now! He dare not allow anyone in the shop with the trap exposed, for there was another chair on the underneath side, which rose as the other descended. If the shop were closed the authorities, with so many rumours afloat, were sure to investigate matters. For some time he sat on a *safe* chair utterly bewildered. He was not addicted to strong liquors, but eventually he rose, and going to his parlour, drank several glasses of brandy in succession.

II

The abode of Mr Oakley in Fore Street has no counterpart in the City today; it was one of those picturesque old houses with small windows and quaint architecture which are dear to all artists; in front the small garden, bright with flowers, did not destroy the commercial aspect denoted by the huge pair of spectacles over the door although the workshop was in the rear.

Soon after the events we have just narrated, a military-looking man in a cloak arrived at the gate, and taking hesitating steps up the pathway, he paused in uncertainty. From the parlour window Johanna Oakley watched the stranger, and thinking she might solve his difficulty, she went out and asked if she could assist him. Her beauty and deep melancholy made an instant impression on him, and he enquired if she was Miss Oakley.

'Yes,' she replied, turning a shade paler, 'tell me, have you come about Mark? You look serious – don't tell me any evil has befallen him. He was to have been here three days ago, but he never came. Have you come from him?'

'I have not come from him, Miss Oakley. I am Colonel Jefferey, his friend; and knowing that this was his destination, and that he carried articles of great value – for he returned from India an affluent man – I have come to tell you all I know of his movements, and consider with you what steps should be taken to trace him. After leaving the ship in the river he went with his black servant to a barber's in Fleet Street. His man waited outside, but he never saw his master again. The barber told him Mark had gone, but the man says that is impossible.'

'Hush! Here comes my mother,' said Johanna, 'she had better not see you yet. Conceal yourself behind this curtain.'

Mr Oakley entered with his wife, who, noticing her daughter's distressed appearance, exclaimed, 'Why, child, how pale and ill you look. I must positively speak to Dr Lupin about you.'

'Dr Lupin may be all very well as a parson,' remarked Mr Oakley, 'but I don't see what he can have to do with Johanna looking pale.'

'A pious man takes an interest in everything and everybody,' his wife replied.

'Then he must be the most intolerable bore in existence, and I don't wonder at his being kicked out of people's houses.'

'If the good man has been kicked he glories in it. You would like to see him murdered on account of his holiness, but you won't say as much when he comes to tea this afternoon.'

'What!' exclaimed her husband, 'haven't I told you a hundred times I won't have him in my house?'

'And haven't I told you twice that number that he shall come to tea? I've asked him and he is coming.'

'But, my dear –'

'It's no use your talking. Oh, dear!' she gasped, 'you have brought on a palpitation – you always do. I must have some brandy.'

'Poor girl,' thought Mr Oakley, as he followed her from the room, 'she has been a good wife, although she has changed of late. I ought to be more considerate.'

Colonel Jefferey reappeared at Johanna's behest, and with a sad heart she heard the story of Mark's adventures, and his disappearance whilst on his way to present her with the pearls.

She cared nothing for the pearls, she said; she would rather have Mark than all the pearls in the world, and in order to learn how the Colonel's efforts progressed she agreed to meet him in Temple Gardens that day week at six o'clock if nothing transpired previously.

As he was about to depart, Johanna exclaimed, 'Dr Lupin! How unfortunate!' and the Colonel again retired behind the curtain.

'Yes, maiden,' said Lupin, 'I am that chosen vessel whom the profane call "Mealy Mouth". I come hither at the bidding of thy respected mother to partake of a vain mixture which rejoiceth in the name of tea.'

'Allow me to pass, if you please, Dr Lupin.'

'Thou art disrespectful considering the honour intended for thee. Thy mother has intended thee to be my wedded wife,' and the slimy hypocrite approached her with extended arms.

'Hands off, or you'll repent it!' exclaimed Johanna.

He still persisted, and the sound of Miss Oakley's alarm proved too much for Colonel Jefferey's self-control; he rushed from his concealment and belaboured the reverend gentleman with the scabbard of his sword with great heartiness. Then, leaving Dr Lupin roaring, and holding a black eye, he escaped out of the door while Johanna locked it after him.

III

A few doors up Bell Yard, at the end of Fleet Street, there was about this time a noted pie-shop kept by a Mrs Lovett, whose wares were in such request by lawyer's clerks and sundry others that at certain hours the place was positively besieged by crowds of epicures who swore there were no pies like them. Tobias often had a pie there when a customer gave him a tip, but it puzzled him how his master knew of it.

One afternoon a shabbily-dressed young man presented himself in the shop, and before he could say anything, Mrs Lovett told him to go away as she never gave anything to beggars.

'I'm not a beggar, marm,' he said, 'I've been unfortunate and I'm looking out for a situation. I hoped you might be able to give me one.'

'What, a dilapidated creature like you!'

'That's where you're wrong, marm; it's manners not togs that make the gentleman. It ain't long ago that I kept my own vehicle.'

'Indeed!'

'Yes, I had the best barrow of greens that ever came out of Clare Market, but some villain sneaked it, and I haven't recovered – but I shall.'

'According to what I see of you if ever you are prosperous your insolence will be unbearable. But what employment could I give you except pie-making? What do you know of that?'

'Oh, I was with a baker for four months – I could soon learn your ways.'

Mrs Lovett looked thoughtful. 'I have a man already, but if I give you a trial can you furnish me with a character?'

'A character? No one knows me. The baker died, and I lost the rest when I lost my barrow.'

'No one knows you? Well, come tomorrow morning and I'll show you what to do.'

In the morning he arrived, and in answer to Mrs Lovett, said his name was Jarvis Williams. Raising a trap-door behind the shop she pointed to some stone stairs: 'By this passage, Jarvis, we descend to the furnace and the ovens, where I will show you how to make the pies, feed the fires, and make yourself generally useful.'

They descended into the bakehouse, a gloomy cellar of vast dimensions and sepulchral appearance; a fitful glare issued from various low-arched entrances in which an oven was placed, and there was a counter with pies on a tray.

'I suppose I'm to have someone to help me in this situation,' said Jarvis. 'One pair of hands could never do the work of such a place.'

'Aren't you satisfied?'

'Oh, yes, only you spoke about having a man.'

'He has gone to his friends – to some of his oldest friends, who will be glad to see him. So now say the word, and let me know if you have any scruples.'

'No scruples, but one objection. I should like to leave when I please.'

'Make your mind easy on that score,' replied Mrs Lovett, 'I never keep anybody many hours after they are dissatisfied. As long as you are industrious you will get on well, but as soon as you begin to get idle and neglect my orders you will receive a piece of information that may –'

'May what?'

'There is no occasion for it yet, but after a time, when you get well fed you may need it, and then you will go to your old friends. Now I must leave you.'

'What a queer way of talking that woman has,' thought Jarvis, 'she seems to have a double meaning all the time. And what a singular-looking place too – nothing visible but darkness. It would be unbearable if it wasn't for the pies.'

Jarvis was at liberty to help himself to as many as he liked, but circumstances blunted his appetite, and before long he discovered he was a prisoner in the gloomy vault. The iron-cased doors above defied all his efforts to escape, and day by day his hopes grew less, until one day he heard strange sounds on the other side of the wall, which he apprehended to be evil. He waited in trepidation as the sounds grew more distinct, and after much suspense a part of the wall gave way, and through the aperture appeared a face – the face of Mr Parmine.

'Who are you?' demanded Jarvis boldly.

'I am the victim of a murderer,' said Mr Parmine, 'and if you are not in league with him you will help me to escape.'

'I should be only too glad to escape myself, for I've been a prisoner for days.'

'Then it's no use my coming in to you, so you had better join me and we will get out somehow. These vaults are no doubt connected with St Dunstan's if we can find its direction.'

'I can tell you that. This is Bell Yard; so turn your back on it and you look towards St Dunstan's.'

'Then come quickly, for I hear footsteps.'

IV

When Sweeney recovered somewhat from his agitation he decided that his only hope of temporary safety depended upon his ability to restore the trap-door to its former condition. He had a certain amount of mechanical skill, but he was handicapped by lack of suitable implements; still he worked at it until far into the night, and although he could not restore its original action, he contrived to fix it so that it would remain rigid under a man's weight.

Then thoroughly exhausted by mental and bodily fatigue, he threw himself upon a couch and slept for some hours. As soon as he was thoroughly awake he arose, and sliding back a panel in the wall he descended many stairs until he reached a vault beneath the trap-door where he expected to find his victims with their brains dashed out. *They were gone!* and not a trace of them to be seen except some blood upon the stones.

Sweeney was aghast – he could only think the worst. Had Mrs Lovett been there?

Mrs Lovett was his mistress and partner in crime, but no one ever saw them together, for his house backed on to hers, and they met by means of mysterious underground passages entirely unknown to the outer world. By a passage known only to himself and his paramour, he made his way towards the pie-shop, and manipulating a secret spring he caused the wall to open like a door, and he entered the bakehouse.

Sweeney had developed a habit of talking to himself: 'I have too many enemies to be safe. I will dispose of them one by one, till no evidence remains against me. My first step must be to stop the tongue of Tobias Wragg. I need not take his life, for that may be of use to me later; but confinement in a lunatic asylum will silence him. Mrs Lovett, too, grows scrupulous and dissatisfied. I've watched her for some time and fear she intends mischief. A little poison when next she visits me may remove any unpleasantness in that direction. Ha! Who –'

Sweeney turned and saw Mrs Lovett at his elbow, and she was in a very bad temper.

'Sweeney Todd!' said Mrs Lovett in a hard voice.

'Well!' replied Sweeney calmly.

'Since I discover that you intend treachery, I demand my share of the plunder this instant – an equal share of the results of our bloodshed.'

'You shall have it,' said Sweeney, with indifference.

'I mean to,' she almost shrieked, 'every penny!'

'Well, all right, be patient. But don't forget that you are greatly in my debt. Remember that I set you up in business – that I taught you the trade secret' – here he drew his fingers significantly across his throat – 'I have kept you in clothes –'

'Clothes!'

'Yes, and you have kept all the profits of the pie-shop, and they belong to me –'

'You want to rob me,' she screamed, 'but I will show you that I will have my due'; and suddenly drawing a knife, she said, 'Now, villain, the whole of the wealth that blood has purchased for me, or I'll slaughter you where you stand!'

'Fool! you should know that Sweeney Todd always calculates his chances,' and springing backwards he drew a pistol from his breast and fired, and Mrs Lovett fell.

'Now the furnace can consume the body and destroy the evidence of any guilt,' he muttered as he opened the furnace door and thrust the body into it.

Immediately the deed was done Todd saw that he had precipitated the end, for the swarm of disappointed pie-eaters would certainly cause an enquiry to be made. How long could he remain with safety?

V

During the next few days Todd was away a great deal, and Tobias was left in charge of the shop, with instructions to do the best he could, and keep his tongue under control. One day, whilst alone, he was startled to hear strange sounds in the barber's parlour (which, of course, was locked in his absence), and still more amazed when the face of Jarvis Williams emerged.

'Phew! out at last,' he exclaimed. 'Why, Toby, old chum, just fancy dropping on you. My word, I have had a time. Where's Todd?'

They were old acquaintances, both hailing from Clare Market; so Jarvis imparted to Tobias the story of his adventures, including what he had heard from Mr Parmine, who had endeavoured to escape by way of St Dunstan's, and also that he had witnessed the murder of Mrs Lovett, whose pies were made of human flesh – poor Tobias felt very sick when he heard that. In return, Tobias gave him the story of Mark Ingestre, the hat, stick, casket, and black servant, and was giving other incidents when Sweeney returned.

Master Williams moved towards the door. 'Well?' said Sweeney questionably. 'It's all right,' said Jarvis. 'I came to see if my father was here, but he's gone,' and away he went. Sweeney looked after him doubtingly; then turning to Tobias he demanded what '*that* fellow' wanted, only to receive the same answer.

'Who else has been?'

'Colonel Jefferey and the black servant kept coming.'

'What did you tell them?'

'Nothing, except that you were out, and I didn't know when you would return.'

'Are you sure that was all?'

'Yes; I never said a word about the things left behind, or the gold casket you had.'

'I *had*, villain!' yelled Todd, and in a burst of ungovernable fury he seized a knife and sprang after his apprentice, who dodged round tables and chairs in terror. But Sweeney heard the rattling of a coach on the cobbles cease at his door: he was evidently expecting it, for he put up the knife and opened the door. 'I'll let you off this time – come, we'll go for a ride. Get in,' he said, pointing to the coach; but Tobias, afraid, refused to move, so Todd called the driver, and the boy's chance of dodging was ended.

They rode to a private mad-house at Peckham, kept by a man named Jonas Fogg, with whom Todd had had previous transactions, and who appeared to know what was expected of him. Todd had some conversation with Fogg, explaining that Tobias suffered from delusions, and was liable to make dangerous statements concerning himself, but he hoped that twelve months' treatment in Fogg's humane institution would restore him to reason, and for that period Todd would pay in advance. Having arranged everything, Sweeney departed, while poor Tobias was taken before the master who caused him to be put in a dark cell, and into a strait jacket if he offered any resistance.

While Fogg was rubbing his hands with satisfaction at receiving twelve months' keep for a patient *who might die in two months*, he little thought how this event would terminate.

When Jarvis Williams left Todd's shop he felt uneasy about Tobias, and he hovered near the shop considering. Soon he saw a coach of ominous appearance arrive, and, later, Tobias was bundled into it and it rumbled away.

Londoners of that day were capable pedestrians, having to depend on their legs for the accomplishment of their travels, and Jarvis thought nothing of following the coach to its destination. For some time it crawled, but afterwards the pace mended, and a journey of about four miles saw the end.

When Sweeney came out alone, Jarvis set off at a good speed towards Clare Market, where some of the toughest rascals in London were to be found, and gathering nearly a score of them they started to the rescue of Tobias.

A leisurely journey to Peckham enabled them to arrange plans *en route*.

It was an awkward place to enter without permission – high walls had to be scaled if they could not gain access from the front door, and that had a grating in it through which a porter scrutinised all visitors. Fortunately the names of the establishment and its proprietor were prominently displayed outside, so Jarvis, having arranged his gang in crouching attitudes where they could not been seen from inside, rang the bell.

'What do you want?' said a voice through the grating.

'Mr Sweeney Todd sent me with an urgent message for Mr Fogg, and I would like to see him,' said Jarvis.

After a brief delay and sounds of bolts and chains being withdrawn, the door opened; Jarvis stepped inside and immediately a desperate rush swept the porter off his feet, and, notwithstanding his strength, he was tied up, legs and arms, before he could resist. Fogg, hearing the noise, put his head out of his room, and they swooped down on him, demanding that Tobias should be produced at once. Fogg, although terrified, tried to equivocate, but they handled him so roughly that he shouted for his attendants, and as they appeared, one by one, they were overpowered, and Tobias was released.

The money Todd had paid was lying on the table, and Fogg would have conveyed it to his pocket if a blow on his hand with a cudgel had not interfered with his plans and allowed his visitors to pocket it instead. They successfully hunted for refreshments, and then, after ransacking the place and releasing all the unfortunate inmates, they left Fogg and his satellites bound hand and foot and departed. Their offence was a hanging one in those days, but they felt certain they need not fear Jonas Fogg.

VI

The figures of Adam and Eve on St Dunstan's Church were striking the hour of six when Colonel Jefferey arrived in Temple Gardens to keep his appointment with Johanna Oakley. She was already there, pale and beautiful, and trembling with anxiety. Unfortunately the Colonel could add but little to what she already knew; he could only tell her of several uneventful visits to the barber's, although he was convinced that Todd could unravel the mystery, and he added that he was in communication with an expert crime investigator.

Johanna thanked him in spite of his ill-success, and she

looked so lovely in her distress that the Colonel decided in the event of Mark never returning to strain all his energies to make her his own; but he was a man of honour and a true friend, and while there was the slightest hope remaining he would not relax his efforts on her behalf. They walked together to Fleet Street, and as she would not accept his offer to escort her home, they parted opposite Todd's shop. The Colonel was going towards Bow Street when a mysterious voice muttered in his ear, 'You seek news of a missing friend; if you will come with me I may be able to help you,' and turning he saw an individual whose features were concealed by a mask.

'I must first know who and what you are before I consent to be guided by a man who hides his features behind a mask,' said the Colonel.

'I wear this mask for other purposes than concealment,' said the man, 'but since you distrust me I will leave you and you will remain without the information you desire.'

'Stay, friend, have you no token to prove your sincerity?'

'Yes, and one that will appeal to you,' he replied, at the same time putting the casket of pearls into his hand.

'Good heavens!' he exclaimed, 'This convinces me – where do you wish me to go?'

'To the shop of Sweeney Todd, the barber, where you will learn something that will surprise you.'

The shop, being only a few yards away, was soon reached, and Colonel Jefferey received the surprise he was promised, for the shop was occupied by constables, and the stranger, removing his mask, revealed the malignant features of Sweeney Todd. The barber, pointing to the Colonel said, 'This is the man who murdered Mark Ingestre, and if you search him you will find the casket of pearls in his possession.'

Colonel Jefferey was astounded; but as the constables gathered round he held out the casket.

'There is no necessity for searching. That villain handed them to me in the street just now as a guarantee of good faith, telling me that if I would visit this shop with him the mystery of Mark Ingestre's disappearance would be cleared up. If Mark has been murdered he is the murderer.'

'You may have a satisfactory explanation,' said the leader of the constables, 'but this is a murder charge, and it is my duty to take you before a magistrate.'

'I am quite ready,' said the Colonel.

Sweeney was chuckling to himself over his cleverness, when the officer said, 'You must come as well.'

'Of course,' replied Sweeney, 'but I'll follow on as I have something to do first.'

'You will come now; there is a counter-charge of murder against you.'

'Nonsense!' said Sweeney, 'why, I've handed the murderer over to you. I'll come on as a witness afterwards.'

'Bring him along!'

And Sweeney joined the party with a constable holding each of his arms.

Let us now refer to certain matters that may seem to require explanation. The Church of St Dunstan's (it was pulled down and rebuilt 1831-3) was an ancient affair that stood 30 feet south of the present church, and beneath it there were extensive underground passages and vaults stretching away in various directions, which few people had ever heard of or suspected to exist. Sweeney Todd, by accident, made the discovery, and after many nocturnal explorations, he concluded that they were entirely forgotten, and that it was safe for him to use them for his own purposes.

A conversation with a skilful mechanic gave him the idea of the trap-door, which they made between them, and when it was completed Sweeney tested its efficiency upon the unsuspecting mechanic, and became the sole possessor of the secret. He worked cautiously, murdering many, and grew rich, but the disposal of the bodies troubled him, as he had to bury them beneath the stones underground.

He had been intimate with Mrs Lovett for some time when he discovered that a passage could be made to communicate with a shop in Bell's Yard, and he installed her in it as an expert pie manufacturer. Then the horrible idea occurred to him that it would be both profitable and expedient if she used the flesh of the dead for her pies, and if any of their assistants suspected anything – *they went to their friends*.

At last the mechanism of the death-trap failed, and Mr

Parmine escaped, because of its irregular action, instead of throwing him on his head, caused him to turn a somersault and fall on his feet, sustaining only minor injuries.

Sweeney Todd prided himself upon his cunning, but little he dreamt what it would do for him. He expected to be at liberty to depart after giving evidence against Colonel Jefferey, but both were detained until the morning. This was a bitter disappointment to Sweeney, who had everything ready for a flight which, during his frequent absences, he had arranged with the captain of a ship in the Thames, who was to sail about midnight – and time and tide wait for no man.

When they appeared before the magistrate Sweeney had a shock which paralysed him with terror; for there, seated beside the magistrate, was the murdered Mr Parmine, and confronting him were Tobias Wragg, Jarvis Williams, Mark Ingestre's black servant, and the captain of the ship he was to have sailed in. It seemed that constables and watchmen had been keeping an eye on Todd, and he was aware of it; and in order to gain the few hours he required to join the ship he endeavoured to betray Colonel Jefferey, but with a fatal result to himself. Every word that went to clear the Colonel struck a blow at Sweeney, with the result that he was committed for trial at the Old Bailey, while Colonel Jefferey went free.

When the trial opened, Sweeney was staggered to see the murdered Mark Ingestre sitting with Colonel Jefferey, and the effect on his nerves was disastrous. It was stated that Mark would have appeared before, but he was too badly injured to be moved, and that but for the defect in the trap he would have been killed. He owed his escape to Mr Parmine.

The evidence of Mark Ingestre and his black servant, of Tobias Wragg, Jarvis Williams, Mr Parmine, and others was overwhelming, and when the judge pronounced sentence of death Sweeney was in a state of abject collapse, from which he never recovered.

His hanging was a great event, for the public were more bitter against him than any other malefactor on record, and especially violent were those who found themselves unwitting cannibals through his instrumentality, and he was pelted all the way to the gallows, his escort having great difficulty in preventing the mob from tearing him limb from limb.

It is satisfactory to record that Mark and Johanna had a happy time in store, and that Fortune was kind to the others who deserved it. Being parted from his treasure embittered Todd's last hours, but it probably did good elsewhere, for Jarvis Williams appeared abundantly supplied with money, possibly due to his subterranean investigations, and by his instrumentality Tobias and his mother were installed in the pie-shop, which they thereafter conducted in exemplary style.

The Reanimated Englishman

by MARY SHELLEY

It may be remembered, that on the fourth of July last, a paragraph appeared in the papers importing that Dr Hotham, of Northumberland, returning from Italy, over Mount St Gothard, a score or two of years ago, had dug out from under an avalanche, in the neighbourhood of the mountain, a human being whose animation had been suspended by the action of the frost. Upon the application of the usual remedies, the patient was resuscitated, and discovered himself to be Mr Dodsworth, the son of the antiquary Dodsworth, who perished in the reign of Charles I. He was thirty-seven years of age at the time of his inhumation, which had taken place as he was returning from Italy, in 1654. It was added that as soon as he was sufficiently recovered he would return to England, under the protection of his preserver. We have since heard no more of him and various plans for public benefit, which have started in philanthropic minds on reading the statement, have already returned to their pristine nothingness. The antiquarian society had eaten their way to several votes for medals, and had already begun, in idea, to consider what prices it could afford to offer for Mr Dodsworth's old clothes, and to conjecture what treasures in the way of pamphlet, old song, or autographic letter his pockets might contain. Poems from all quarters, of all kinds, elegiac, congratulatory, burlesque and allegoric, were half written. Mr Godwin had suspended for the sake of such authentic information the history of the Commonwealth he had just begun. It is hard not only that the world should be baulked of these destined gifts from the talents of the country, but also that it should be promised and then deprived of a new subject of romantic wonder and scientific interest. A novel idea is worth much in the commonplace routine of life, but a new fact, an astonishment, a miracle, a palpable wandering from the course of things into apparent impossibilities, is a circumstance to which the imagination must cling with delight, and we say again that it is hard, very hard, that Mr Dodsworth refuses to appear, and that the believers in his resuscitation are forced to undergo the sarcasms and triumphant arguments of those sceptics who always keep on the safe side of the hedge.

Now we do not believe that any contradiction or impossibility is attached to the adventures of this youthful antique. Animation (I believe physiologists agree) can as easily be suspended for a hundred or two years, as for as many seconds. A body hermetically sealed up by the frost, is of necessity preserved in its pristine entireness. That which is totally secluded from the action of external agency, can neither have any thing added to nor taken away from it: no decay can take place, for something can never become nothing; under the influence of that state of being which we call death, change but not annihilation removes from our sight the corporeal atoma; the earth receives sustenance from them, the air is fed by them, each element takes its own, thus seizing forcible repayment of what it had lent. But the elements that hovered round Mr Dodsworth's icy shroud had no power to overcome the obstacle it presented. No zephyr could gather a hair from his head, nor could the influence of dewy night or genial morn penetrate his more than adamantine panoply. The story of the Seven Sleepers rests on a miraculous interposition – they slept. Mr Dodsworth did not sleep; his breast never heaved, his pulses were stopped; death had his finger pressed on his lips which no breath might pass. He has removed it now, the grim shadow is vanquished, and stands wondering. His victim has cast from him the frosty spell, and arises as perfect a man as he had lain down a hundred and fifty years before. We have eagerly desired to be furnished with some particulars of his first conversations, and the mode in which he has learnt to adapt himself to his new scene of life. But since facts are denied to us, let us be permitted to indulge in conjecture. What his first words were may be guessed from the expressions used by people exposed to shorter accidents of the like nature. But as his powers return, the plot thickens. His dress had already excited Doctor Hotham's astonishment – the peaked beard – the love locks – the frill, which, until it was thawed, stood stiff under the mingled influence of starch and frost; his dress fashioned like that of one of Vandyke's portraits, or (a more familiar similitude) Mr Sapio's costume in Winter's Opera of the Oracle, his pointed shoes – all spoke of other times. The curiosity of his preserver was keenly awake, that of Mr Dodsworth was about to be roused. But to be enabled to conjecture with any degree of likelihood the tenor of his first inquiries, we must endeavour to make out what part he played in his former life. He lived at the most interesting period of English history – he was lost to the world when Oliver Cromwell had arrived at the summit of his ambition, and in the eyes of all Europe the Commonwealth of England appeared so established as to endure for ever. Charles I was dead; Charles II was an outcast, a beggar, bankrupt even in hope. Mr Dodsworth's father, the antiquary, received a salary from the republican general, Lord Fairfax, who was himself a great lover of antiquities, and died the very year that his son went to his long, but not unending sleep, a curious coincidence this, for it would seem that our frost-preserved friend was returning to England on his father's death, to claim probably his inheritance – how short-lived are human views! Where now is Mr Dodsworth's patrimony? Where his co-heirs, executors, and fellow legatees? His protracted absence has, we should suppose, given the present possessors to his estate – the world's chronology is a hundred and seventy years older since he seceded from the busy scene, hands after hands have tilled his acres, and then become clods beneath them; we may be permitted to doubt whether one single particle of their surface is individually the same as those which were to have been his – the youthful soil would of itself reject the antique clay of its claimant.

Mr Dodsworth, if we may judge from the circumstance of his being abroad, was no zealous commonwealth's man yet his having chosen Italy as the country in which to make his tour and his projected return to England on his father's death, renders it probable that he was no violent loyalist. One of those men he seems to be (or have been) who did not follow Cato's advice as recorded in the Pharsalia; a party, if to be of no party admits of such a term, which Dante recommends us utterly to despise, and which not unseldom falls between the two stools, a seat on either of which is so carefully avoided. Still Mr Dodsworth could hardly fail to feel anxious for the latest news from his native country at so critical a period; his absence might have put his own property in jeopardy; we may imagine therefore that after his limbs had felt the cheerful return of circulation, and after he had refreshed himself with such of earth's products as from all analogy he never could have hoped to live to eat, after he had been told from what peril he had been rescued, and said a prayer thereon which even appeared enormously long to Dr Hotham – we may imagine, we say, that his first question would be: 'If any news had arrived lately from England?'

'I had letters yesterday,' Dr Hotham may well be supposed to reply.

'Indeed,' cries Mr Dodsworth, 'and pray, sir, has any change for better or worse occurred in that poor distracted country?'

Dr Hotham suspects a Radical, and coldly replies: 'Why, sir, it would be difficult to say in what its distraction consists. People talk of starving manufacturers, bankruptcies, and the fall of the Joint Stock Companies – excrescences these, excrescences which will attach themselves to a state of full health. England, in fact, was never in a more prosperous condition.'

Mr Dodsworth now more than suspects the Republican, and, with what we have supposed to be his accustomed caution, sinks for a while his loyalty, and in a moderate tone asks: 'Do our governors look with careless eyes upon the symptoms of over-health?'

'Our governors,' answers his preserver, 'if you mean our ministry, are only too alive to temporary embarrassment.' (We beg Doctor Hotham's pardon if we wrong him in making him a high Tory; such a quality appertains to our pure anticipated cognition of a Doctor, and such is the only cognizance that we have of this gentleman.) 'It were to be wished that they showed themselves more firm – the king, God bless him!'

'Sir!' exclaims Mr Dodsworth.

Doctor Hotham continues, not aware of the excessive astonishment exhibited by his patient: 'The king, God bless him, spares immense sums from his privy purse for the relief of his subjects, and his example has been imitated by all the aristocracy and wealth of England.'

'The King!' ejaculates Mr Dodsworth.

'Yes, sir,' emphatically rejoins his preserver; 'the king, and I am happy to say that the prejudices that so unhappily and unwarrantably possessed the English people with regard to his Majesty are now, with a few' (with added severity) 'and I may say contemptible exceptions, exchanged for dutiful love and such reverence as his talents, virtues, and paternal care deserve.'

'Dear sir, you delight me,' replies Mr Dodsworth, while his loyalty late a tiny bud suddenly expands into full flower; 'yet I hardly understand; the change is so sudden; and the man – Charles Stuart, King Charles, I may now call him, his murder is I trust execrated as it deserves?'

Dr Hotham put his hand on the pulse of his patient – he feared an access of delirium from such a wandering from the subject. The pulse was calm, and Mr Dodsworth continued: 'That unfortunate martyr looking down from heaven is, I trust, appeased by the reverence paid to his name and the prayers dedicated to his memory. No sentiment, I think I may venture to assert, is so general in England as the compassion and love in which the memory of that hapless monarch is held?'

'And his son, who now reigns?—'

'Surely, sir, you forget; no son; that of course is impossible. No descendant of his fills the English throne, now worthily occupied by the house of Hanover. The despicable race of the Stuarts, long outcast and wandering, is now extinct, and the last days of the last Pretender to the crown of that family justified in the eyes of the world the sentence which ejected it from the kingdom for ever.'

Such must have been Mr Dodsworth's first lesson in politics. Soon, to the wonder of the preserver and preserved, the real state of the case must have been revealed; for a time, the strange and tremendous circumstance of his long trance may have threatened the wits of Mr Dodsworth with a total overthrow. He had, as he crossed Mount

Saint Gothard, mourned a father – now every human being he had ever seen is 'lapped in lead,' is dust, each voice he had ever heard is mute. The very sound of the English tongue is changed, as his experience in conversation with Dr Hotham assures him. Empires, religions, races of men, have probably sprung up or faded; his own patrimony (the thought is idle yet, without it, how can he live?) is sunk into the thirsty gulf that gapes ever greedy to swallow the past; his learning, his acquirements, are probably obsolete; with a bitter smile he thinks to himself, I must take to my father's profession, and turn antiquary. The familiar objects, thoughts, and habits of my boyhood, are now antiquities. He wonders where the hundred and sixty folio volumes of MS that his father had compiled, and which, as a lad, he had regarded with religious reverence, now are – where – ah, where? His favourite playmate, the friend of his later years, his destined and lovely bride; tears long frozen are uncongealed, and flow down his young old cheeks.

But we do not wish to be pathetic; surely since the days of the patriarchs, no fair lady had her death mourned by her lover so many years after it had taken place. Necessity, tyrant of the world, in some degree reconciles Mr Dodsworth to his fate. At first he is persuaded that the later generation of man is much deteriorated from his contemporaries; they are neither so tall, so handsome, nor so intelligent. Then by degrees he begins to doubt his first impression. The ideas that had taken possession of his brain before his accident, and which had been frozen up for so many years, begin to thaw and dissolve away, making room for others. He dresses himself in the modern style, and does not object much to anything except the neck-cloth and hardboarded hat. He admires the texture of his shoes and stockings, and looks with admiration on a small Genevese watch, which he often consults, as if he were not yet assured that time had made progress in its accustomed manner, and as if he should find on its dial plate occular demonstration that he had exchanged his thirty-seventh year for his two hundredth upwards, and had left AD 1654 far behind to find himself suddenly a beholder of the ways of men in this enlightened nineteenth century. His curiosity is insatiable; when he reads, his eyes cannot purvey fast enough to his mind, and every now and then he lights upon some inexplicable passage, some discovery and knowledge familiar to us, but undreamed of in his days, that throws him into wonder and interminable reverie. Indeed, he may be supposed to pass much of his time in that state, now and then interupting himself with a royalist song against old Noll and the Roundheads, breaking off suddenly, and looking round fearfully to see who were his auditors, and on beholding the modern appearance of his friend the Doctor, sighing to think that it is no longer of import to any, whether he sing a cavalier catch or a puritanic psalm.

It were an endless task to develop all the philosophic ideas to which Mr Dodsworth's resuscitation naturally gives birth. We should like much to converse with this gentleman, and still more to observe ~~the progress of his mind, and the change of his ideas in his very novel~~ situation. If he be a sprightly youth, fond of the shows of the world, careless of the higher human pursuits, he may proceed summarily to cast into the shade all trace of his former life, and endeavour to merge himself at once into the stream of humanity now flowing. It would be curious enough to observe the mistakes he would make, and the medley of manners which would thus be produced. He may think to enter into active life, become whig or tory as his inclinations lead, and get a seat in the, even to him, once called chapel of St Stephens. He may content himself with turning contemplative philosopher, and find sufficient food for his mind in tracing the march of the human intellect, the changes which have been wrought in the dispositions, desires, and powers of mankind. Will he be an advocate for perfectibility or deterioration? He must admire our manufactures, the progress of science, the diffusion of knowledge, and the fresh spirit of enterprise characteristic of our countrymen. Will he find any individuals to be compared to the glorius spirits of the day? Moderate in his views as we have supposed him to be, he will probably fall at once into the temporising tone of mind now so much in vogue. He will be pleased to find a calm in politics; he will greatly admire the ministry who have succeeded in conciliating almost all parties – to find peace where he left feud. The same character which he bore a couple of hundred years ago, will influence him now; he will still be the moderate, peaceful, unenthusiastic Mr Dodsworth that he was in 1647.

For notwithstanding education and circumstances may suffice to direct and form the rough material of the mind, it cannot create, nor give intellect, noble aspiration, and energetic constancy where dulness, wavering of purpose, and grovelling desires, are stamped by nature. Entertaining this belief we have (to forget Mr Dodsworth for awhile) often made conjectures how such and such heroes of antiquity would act, if they were reborn in these times: and then awakened fancy has gone on to imagine that some of them are reborn; that according to the theory explained by Virgil in his sixth Aeneid, every thousand years the dead return to life, and their souls endued with the same sensibilities and capacities as before, are turned naked of knowledge into this world, again to dress their skeleton powers in such habiliments as situation, education, and experience will furnish. Pythagoras, we are told, remembered many transmigrations of this sort, as having occurred to himself, though for a philosopher he made very little use of his anterior memories. It would prove an instructive school for kings and statesmen, and in fact for all human beings, called on as they are, to play their part on the stage of the world, could they remember what they had been. Thus we might obtain a glimpse of heaven and of hell, as, the secret of our former identity confined to our own bosoms, we winced or exulted in the blame or praise bestowed on our former selves. While the love of glory and posthumous reputation is as natural to man as his attachment to life itself, he must be, under such a state of things, tremblingly alive to the historic records of his honour or shame. The mild spirit of Fox would have been soothed by the recollection that he had played a worthy part as Marcus Antoninus – the former experiences of Alcibiades or even of the emasculated Steeny of James I might have caused Sheridan to have refused to tread over again the same path of dazzling but fleeting brilliancy. The soul of our modern Corinna would have been purified and exalted by a consciousness that once it had given life to the form of Sappho. If at the present moment the witch, memory, were in a freak, to cause all the present generation to recollect that some ten centuries back they had been somebody else, would not several of our free-thinking martyrs wonder to find that they had suffered as Christians under Domitian, while the judge as he passed sentence would suddenly become aware, that formerly he had condemned the saints of the early church to the torture, for not renouncing the religion he now upheld – nothing but benevolent actions and real goodness would come pure out of the ordeal. While it would be whimsical to perceive how some great men in parish affairs would strut under the consciousness that their hands had once held a sceptre, an honest artizan or pilfering domestic would find that he was little altered by being transformed into an idle noble or director of a joint stock company; in every way we may suppose that the humble would be exalted, and the noble and the proud would feel their stars and honours dwindle into baubles and child's play when they called to mind the lowly stations they had once occupied. If philosophical novels were in fashion, we conceive an excellent one might be written on the development of the same mind in various stations, in different periods of the world's history.

But to return to Mr Dodsworth, and indeed with a few more words to bid him farewell. We entreat him no longer to bury himself in obscurity; or, if he modestly decline publicity, we beg him to make himself known personally to us. We have a thousand inquiries to make, doubts to clear up, facts to ascertain. If any fear that old habits and strangeness of appearance will make him ridiculous to those accustomed to associate with modern exquisites, we beg to assure him that we are not given to ridicule mere outward shows, and that worth and intrinsic excellence will always claim our respect.

This we say, if Mr Dodsworth is alive. Perhaps he is again no more. Perhaps he opened his eyes only to shut them again more obstinately; perhaps his ancient clay could not thrive on the harvests of these latter days. After a little wonder; a little shuddering to find himself the dead alive – finding no affinity between himself and the present state of things – he has bidden once more an eternal farewell to the sun. Followed to his grave by his preserver and the wondering villagers, he may sleep the true death-sleep in the same valley where he so long reposed. Doctor Hotham may have erected a simple tablet over his twice-buried remains, inscribed:

To the Memory of R. Dodsworth,
An Englishman,
Born April 1, 1617; Died July 16, 1826; Aged 209.

An inscription which, if it were preserved during any terrible convulsion that caused the world to begin its life again, would occasion many learned disquisitions and ingenious theories concerning a race which authentic records showed to have secured the privilege of attaining so vast an age.

The Vampyre

JOHN POLIDORI

IT HAPPENED THAT in the midst of the dissipations attendant
upon a London winter, there appeared at the various parties of
the leaders of the *ton* a nobleman, more remarkable for his
singularities, than his rank. He gazed upon the mirth around
him, as if he could not participate therein. Apparently, the light
laughter of the fair only attracted his attention, that he might
by a look quell it, and throw fear into those breasts where
thoughtlessness reigned. Those who felt this sensation of awe,
could not explain whence it arose: some attributed it to the dead
grey eye, which fixing upon the object's face, did not seem to
penetrate, and at one glance to pierce through to the inward
workings of the heart; but fell upon the cheek with a leaden ray
that weighed upon the skin it could not pass. His peculiarities
caused him to be invited to every house; all wished to see him,

and those who had been accustomed to violent excitement, and now felt the weight of *ennui*, were pleased at having something in their presence capable of engaging their attention. In spite of the deadly hue of his face, which never gained a warmer tint, either from the blush of modesty, or from the strong emotion of passion, though its form and outline were beautiful, many of the female hunters after notoriety attempted to win his attentions, and gain, at least, some marks of what they might term affection: Lady Mercer, who had been the mockery of every monster shewn in drawing-rooms since her marriage, threw herself in his way, and did all but put on the dress of a mountebank, to attract his notice – though in vain – when she stood before him, though his eyes were apparently fixed upon hers, still it seemed as if they were unperceived – even her un-appalled impudence was baffled, and she left the field. But though the common adultress could not influence even the guid-ance of his eyes, it was not that the female sex was indifferent to him: yet such was the apparent caution with which he spoke to the virtuous wife and innocent daughter, that few knew he ever addressed himself to females. He had, however, the reputation of a winning tongue; and whether it was that it even overcame the dread of his singular character, or that they were moved by his apparent hatred of vice, he was as often among those females who form the boast of their sex from their domestic virtues, as among those who sully it by their vices.

About the same time, there came to London a young gentle-man of the name of Aubrey: he was an orphan left with an only sister in the possession of great wealth, by parents who died while he was yet in childhood. Left also to himself by guardians, who thought it their duty merely to take care of his fortune, while they relinquished the more important charge of his mind to the care of mercenary subalterns, he cultivated more his imagination than his judgment. He had, hence, that high romantic feeling of honour and candour, which daily ruins so many milliners' apprentices. He believed all to sympathise with virtue, and thought that vice was thrown in by Providence merely for the picturesque effect of the scene, as we see in romances: he thought that the misery of a cottage merely consisted in the vesting of clothes, which were warm, but which were better adapted to the painter's eye by their irregular folds and various coloured patches. He thought, in fine, that the dreams of poets were the realities of life. He was handsome, frank, and rich: for these reasons, upon his entering into the gay circles, many mothers surrounded him, striving which should describe with least truth their languishing or romping favourites: the daughters at the same time, by their brightening countenances when he approached, and by their sparkling eyes, when he opened his lips, soon led him into false notions of his talents and his merit. Attached as he was to the romance of his solitary hours, he was startled at finding, that, except in the tallow and wax candles that flickered, not from the presence of a ghost, but from want of snuffing, there was no foundation in real life for any of that congeries of pleasing pictures and descriptions contained in those volumes, from which he had formed his study. Finding, however, some compensation in his gratified vanity, he was about to relinquish his dreams, when the extraordinary being we have above described, crossed him in his career.

He watched him; and the very impossibility of forming an idea of the character of a man entirely absorbed in himself, who gave few other signs of his observation of external objects, than the tacit assent of their existence, implied by the avoidance of their contact: allowing his imagination to picture every thing that flattered its propensity to extravagant ideas, he soon formed this object into the hero of a romance, and determined to observe the offspring of his fancy, rather than the person before him. He became acquainted with him, paid him attentions, and so far advanced upon his notice, that his presence was always recognised. He gradually learnt that Lord Ruthven's affairs were embarrassed, and soon found, from the notes of preparation in —— Street, that he was about to travel. Desirous of gaining some information respecting this singular character, who, till now, had only whetted his curiosity, he hinted to his guardians, that it was time for him to perform the tour, which for many generations has been thought necessary to enable the young to take some rapid steps in the career of vice towards putting themselves upon an equality with the aged, and not allowing them to appear as if fallen from the skies, whenever scandalous intrigues are mentioned as the subjects of pleasantry or of praise, according to the degree of skill shewn in carrying them on. They consented: and Aubrey immediately mentioning his intentions to Lord Ruthven, was surprised to receive from him a proposal to join him. Flattered by such a mark of esteem from him, who, apparently, had nothing in common with other men, he gladly accepted it, and in a few days they had passed the circling waters.

Hitherto, Aubrey had had no opportunity of studying Lord Ruthven's character, and now he found, that, though many more of his actions were exposed to his view, the results offered different conclusions from the apparent motives to his conduct. His companion was profuse in his liberality – the idle, the vagabond, and the beggar, received from his hand more than enough to relieve their immediate wants. But Aubrey could not avoid remarking, that it was not upon the virtuous, reduced to indigence by the misfortunes attendant even upon virtue, that he bestowed his alms – these were sent from the door with hardly suppressed sneers; but when the profligate came to ask something, not to relieve his wants, but to allow him to wallow in his lust, or to sink him still deeper in his iniquity, he was sent away with rich charity. This was, however, attributed by him to the greater importunity of the vicious, which generally prevails over the retiring bashfulness of the virtuous indigent.

There was one circumstance about the charity of his Lordship, which was still more impressed upon his mind: all those upon whom it was bestowed, inevitably found that there was a curse upon it, for they were all either led to the scaffold, or sunk to the lowest and the most abject misery. At Brussels and other towns through which they passed, Aubrey was surprised at the apparent eagerness with which his companion sought for the centres of all fashionable vice; there he entered into all the spirit of the faro table: he betted, and always gambled with success, except where the known sharper was his antagonist, and then he lost even more than he gained; but it was always with the same unchanging face, with which he generally watched the society around: it was not, however, so when he encountered the rash youthful novice, or the luckless father of a numerous family; then his very wish seemed fortune's law – this apparent abstractedness of mind was laid aside, and his eyes sparkled with more fire than that of the cat whilst dallying with the half-dead mouse. In every town, he left the formerly affluent youth, torn from the circle he adorned, cursing, in the solitude of a dungeon, the fate that had drawn him within the reach of this fiend; whilst many a father sat frantic, amidst the speaking looks of mute hungry children, without a single farthing of his late immense wealth, wherewith to buy even sufficient to satisfy their present craving. Yet he took no money from the gambling table; but immediately lost, to the ruiner of many, the last gilder he had just snatched from the convulsive grasp of the innocent: this might but be the result of a certain degree of knowledge, which was not, however, capable of combating the cunning of the more experienced. Aubrey often wished to represent this to his friend, and beg him to resign that charity and pleasure which proved the ruin of all, and did not tend to his own profit; but he delayed it – for each day he hoped his friend would give him some opportunity of speaking frankly and openly to him; however, this never occurred. Lord

Ruthven in his carriage, and amidst the various wild and rich scenes of nature, was always the same: his eye spoke less than his lip; and though Aubrey was near the object of his curiosity, he obtained no greater gratification from it than the constant excitement of vainly wishing to break that mystery, which to his exalted imagination began to assume the appearance of something supernatural.

They soon arrived at Rome, and Aubrey for a time lost sight of his companion; he left him in daily attendance upon the morning circle of an Italian countess, whilst he went in search of the memorials of another almost deserted city. Whilst he was thus engaged, letters arrived from England, which he opened with eager impatience; the first was from his sister, breathing nothing but affection; the others were from his guardians, the latter astonished him; if it had before entered into his imagination that there was an evil power resident in his companion, these seemed to give him almost sufficient reason for the belief. His guardians insisted upon his immediately leaving his friend, and urged, that his character was dreadfully vicious, for that the possession of irresistible powers of seduction, rendered his licentious habits more dangerous to society. It had been discovered, that his contempt for the adultress had not originated in hatred of her character; but that he had required, to enhance his gratification, that his victim, the partner of his guilt, should be hurled from the pinnacle of unsullied virtue, down to the lowest abyss of infamy and degradation: in fine, that all those females whom he had sought, apparently on account of their virtue, had, since his departure, thrown even the mask aside, and had not scrupled to expose the whole deformity of their vices to the public gaze.

Aubrey determined upon leaving one, whose character had not yet shown a single bright point on which to rest the eye. He resolved to invent some plausible pretext for abandoning him altogether, purposing, in the meanwhile, to watch him more closely, and to let no slight circumstances pass by unnoticed. He entered into the same circle, and soon perceived, that his Lordship was endeavouring to work upon the inexperience of the daughter of the lady whose house he chiefly frequented. In Italy, it is seldom that an unmarried female is met with in society; he was therefore obliged to carry on his plans in secret; but Aubrey's eye followed him in all his windings, and soon discovered that an assignation had been appointed, which would most likely end in the ruin of an innocent, though thoughtless girl. Losing no time, he entered the apartment of Lord Ruthven, and abruptly asked him his intentions with respect to the lady, informing him at the same time that he was aware of his being about to meet her that very night. Lord Ruthven answered, that his intentions were such as he supposed all would have upon such an occasion; and upon being pressed whether he intended to marry her, merely laughed. Aubrey retired; and, immediately writing a note, to say, that from that moment he must decline accompanying his Lordship in the remainder of their proposed tour, he ordered his servant to seek other apartments, and calling upon the mother of the lady, informed her of all he knew, not only with regard to her daughter, but also concerning the character of his Lordship. The assignation was prevented. Lord Ruthven next day merely sent his servant to notify his complete assent to a separation; but did not hint any suspicion of his plans having been foiled by Aubrey's interposition.

Having left Rome, Aubrey directed his steps towards Greece, and crossing the Peninsula, soon found himself in Athens. He then fixed his residence in the house of a Greek; and soon occupied himself in tracing the faded records of ancient glory upon monuments that apparently, ashamed of chronicling the deeds of freemen only before slaves, had hidden themselves beneath the sheltering soil or many coloured lichen. Under the same roof as himself, existed a being, so beautiful and delicate, that she might have formed the model for a painter, wishing to portray on canvass the promised hope of the faithful in Mahomet's paradise, save that her eyes spoke too much mind for any one to think she could belong to those who had no souls. As she danced upon the plain, or tripped along the mountain's side, one would have thought the gazelle a poor type of her beauties; for who would have exchanged her eye, apparently the eye of animated nature, for that sleepy luxurious look of the animal suited but to the taste of an epicure. The light step of Ianthe often accompanied Aubrey in his search after antiquities, and often would the unconscious girl, engaged in the pursuit of a Kashmere butterfly, show the whole beauty of her form, floating as it were upon the wind, to the eager gaze of him, who forgot the letters he had just deciphered upon an almost effaced tablet, in the contemplation of her sylph-like figure. Often would her tresses falling, as she flitted around, exhibit in the sun's ray such delicately brilliant and swiftly fading hues, as might well excuse the forgetfulness of the antiquary, who let escape from his mind the very object he had before thought of vital importance to the proper interpretation of a passage in Pausanias. But why attempt to describe charms which all feel, but none can appreciate? It was innocence, youth, and beauty, unaffected by crowded drawing-rooms and stifling balls. Whilst he drew those remains of which he wished to preserve a memorial for his future hours, she would stand by, and watch the magic effects of his pencil, in tracing the scenes of her native place; she would then describe to him the circling dance upon the open plain, would paint to him in all the glowing colours of youthful memory, the marriage pomp she remembered viewing in her infancy; and then, turning to subjects that had evidently made a greater impression upon her mind, would tell him all the supernatural tales of her nurse. Her earnestness and apparent belief of what she narrated, excited the interest even of Aubrey; and often as she told him the tale of the living

Vampyre, who had passed years amidst his friends, and dearest ties, forced every year, by feeding upon the life of a lovely female to prolong his existence for the ensuing months, his blood would run cold, whilst he attempted to laugh her out of such idle and horrible fantasies; but Ianthe cited to him the names of old men, who had at last detected one living among themselves, after several of their near relatives and children had been found marked with the stamp of the fiend's appetite; and when she found him so incredulous, she begged of him to believe her, for it had been remarked, that those who had dared to question their existence, always had some proof given, which obliged them, with grief and heartbreaking, to confess it was true. She detailed to him the traditional appearance of these monsters, and his horror was increased, by hearing a pretty accurate description of Lord Ruthven; he, however, still persisted in persuading her, that there could be no truth in her fears, though at the same time he wondered at the many coincidences which had all tended to excite a belief in the supernatural power of Lord Ruthven.

Aubrey began to attach himself more and more to Ianthe; her innocence, so contrasted with all the affected virtues of the women among whom he had sought for his vision of romance, won his heart; and while he ridiculed the idea of a young man of English habits, marrying an uneducated Greek girl, still he found himself more and more attached to the almost fairy form before him. He would tear himself at times from her, and, forming a plan for some antiquarian research, he would depart, determined not to return until his object was attained; but he always found it impossible to fix his attention upon the ruins around him, whilst in his mind he retained an image that seemed alone the rightful possessor of his thoughts. Ianthe was un-conscious of his love, and was ever the same frank infantile being he had first known. She always seemed to part from him with reluctance; but it was because she had no longer anyone with whom she could visit her favourite haunts, whilst her guardian was occupied in sketching or uncovering some fragment which had yet escaped the destructive hand of time. She had appealed to her parents on the subject of Vampyres, and they both, with several present, affirmed their existence, pale with horror at the very name. Soon after, Aubrey determined to proceed upon one of his excursions, which was to detain him for a few hours; when they heard the name of the place, they all at once begged of him not to return at night, as he must necessarily pass through a wood, where no Greek would ever remain, after the day had closed, upon any consideration. They described it as the resort of the vampyres in their nocturnal orgies, and denounced the most heavy evils as impending upon him who dared to cross their path. Aubrey made light of their representations, and tried to laugh them out of the idea; but when he saw them shudder at his daring thus to mock a superior, infernal power, the very name of which apparently made their blood freeze, he was silent.

Next morning Aubrey set off upon his excursion unattended; he was surprised to observe the melancholy face of his host, and was concerned to find that his words, mocking the belief of those horrible fiends, had inspired them with such terror. When he was about to depart, Ianthe came to the side of his horse, and earnestly begged of him to return, ere night allowed the power of these beings to be put in action – he promised. He was, however, so occupied in his research that he did not perceive that daylight would soon end, and that in the horizon there was one of those specks which, in the warmer climates, so rapidly gather into a tremendous mass, and pour all their rage upon the devoted country. He at last, however, mounted his horse, determined to make up by speed for his delay: but it was too late. Twilight, in these southern climates, is almost unknown; immediately the sun sets, night begins: and ere he had advanced far, the power of the storm was above – its echoing thunders had scarcely an interval of rest – its thick heavy rain forced its way through the canopying foliage, whilst the blue forked lightning seemed to fall and radiate at his very feet. Suddenly his horse took fright, and he was carried with dreadful rapidity through the entangled forest. The animal at last, through fatigue, stopped, and he found, by the glare of lightning, that he was in the neighbourhood of a hovel that hardly lifted itself up from the masses of dead leaves and brushwood which surrounded it. Dismounting, he approached, hoping to find someone to guide him to the town, or at least trusting to obtain shelter from the pelting storm. As he approached, the thunders, for a moment silent, allowed him to hear the dreadful shrieks of a woman mingling with the stifled, exultant mockery of a laugh, continued in one almost unbroken sound – he was startled: but, roused by the thunder which again rolled over his head, he, with a sudden effort, forced open the door of the hut. He found himself in utter darkness: the sound, however, guided him. He was apparently unperceived; for, though he called, still the sounds continued, and no notice was taken of him. He found himself in contact with someone, whom he immediately seized; when a voice cried, 'Again baffled!' to which a loud laugh succeeded; and he felt himself grappled by one whose strength seemed superhuman: determined to sell his life as dearly as he could, he struggled; but it was in vain: he was lifted from his feet and hurled with enormous force against the ground – his enemy threw himself upon him, and kneeling upon his breast, had placed his hands upon his throat – when the glare of many torches penetrating through the hole that gave light in the day, disturbed him – he instantly rose, and, leaving his prey, rushed through the door, and in a moment the crashing of the branches, as he broke through the wood, was no longer heard. The storm was now still; and Aubrey, incapable of moving, was soon heard by those without. They entered; the light of their torches fell upon the mud walls, and the thatch loaded on every individual straw with heavy flakes of soot. At the desire of Aubrey they searched for her who had attracted him by her cries; he was again left in darkness; but what was his horror, when the light of the torches once more burst upon him, to perceive the airy form of his fair conductress brought in a lifeless corpse. He shut his eyes, hoping that it was but a vision arising from his disturbed imagination; but he again saw the same form, when he unclosed them, stretched by his side. There was no colour upon her cheek, not even upon her lip; yet there was a stillness about her face that seemed almost as attaching as the life that once dwelt there – upon her neck and breast was blood, and upon her throat were the marks of teeth having opened the vein – to this the men pointed, crying simultaneously struck with horror, 'A Vampyre! a Vampyre!' A litter was quickly formed, and Aubrey was laid by the side of her who had lately been to him the object of so many bright and fairy visions, now fallen with the flower of life that had died within her. He knew not what his thoughts were – his mind was benumbed and seemed to shun reflection, and take refuge in vacancy – he held almost unconsciously in his hand a naked dagger of a particular construction, which had been found in the hut. They were soon met by different parties who had been engaged in the search of her whom a mother had missed. Their lamentable cries, as they approached the city, forewarned the parents of some dreadful catastrophe. To describe their grief would be impossible; but when they ascertained the cause of their child's death, they looked at Aubrey, and pointed to the corpse. They were inconsolable; both died broken-hearted.

Aubrey being put to bed was seized with a most violent fever, and was often delirious; in these intervals he would call upon Lord Ruthven and upon Ianthe – by some unaccountable combination he seemed to beg of his former companion to spare the being he loved. At other times he would imprecate maledictions upon his head, and curse him as her destroyer. Lord Ruthven chanced at this time to arrive at Athens, and, from whatever motive, upon hearing of the state of Aubrey, immediately placed himself in the same house, and became his constant attendant. When the latter recovered from his delirium, he was horrified and startled at the sight of him whose image he had now combined with that of a Vampyre; but Lord Ruthven, by his kind words, implying almost repentance for the fault that had caused their separation, and still more by the attention, anxiety, and care which he showed, soon reconciled him to his presence. His lordship seemed quite changed; he no longer appeared that apathetic being who had so astonished Aubrey; but as his convalescence began to be rapid, he again gradually retired into the same state of mind, and Aubrey perceived no difference from the former man, except that at times he was surprised to meet his gaze fixed intently upon him, with a smile of malicious exultation playing upon his lips: he knew not why, but this smile haunted him. During the last stage of the invalid's recovery, Lord Ruthven was apparently engaged in watching the tideless waves raised by the cooling breeze, or in marking the progress of those orbs, circling, like our world, the moveless sun – indeed, he appeared to wish to avoid the eyes of all.

Aubrey's mind, by this shock, was much weakened, and that elasticity of spirit which had once so distinguished him now seemed to have fled forever. He was now as much a lover of solitude and silence as Lord Ruthven; but much as he wished for solitude, his mind could not find it in the neighbourhood of Athens; if he sought it amidst the ruins he had formerly frequented, Ianthe's form stood by his side – if he sought it in the woods, her light step would appear wandering amidst the underwood, in quest of the modest violet; then suddenly turning round, would show, to his wild imagination, her pale face and wounded throat, with a meek smile upon her lips. He determined to fly scenes, every feature of which created such bitter associations in his mind. He proposed to Lord Ruthven, to whom he held himself bound by the tender care he had taken of him during his illness, that they should visit those parts of Greece neither had yet seen. They travelled in every direction, and sought every spot to which a recollection could be attached: but though they thus hastened from place to place, yet they seemed not to heed what they gazed upon. They heard much of robbers, but they gradually began to slight these reports, which they imagined were only the invention of individuals, whose interest it was to excite the generosity of those whom they defended from pretended dangers. In consequence of thus neglecting the advice of the inhabitants, on one occasion they travelled with only a few guards, more to serve as guides than as a defence. Upon entering, however, a narrow defile, at the bottom of which was the bed of a torrent, with large masses of rock brought down from the neighbouring precipices, they had reason to repent their negligence; for scarcely were the whole of the party engaged in the narrow pass, when they were startled by the whistling of bullets close to their heads, and by the echoed report of several guns. In an instant their guards had left them, and, placing themselves behind rocks, had begun to fire in the direction whence the report came. Lord Ruthven and Aubrey, imitating their example, retired for a moment behind the sheltering turn of the defile: but ashamed of being thus detained by a foe, who with insulting shouts bade them advance, and being exposed to unresisting slaughter, if any of the robbers should climb above and take them in the rear, they determined at once to rush forward in search of the enemy. Hardly had they lost the shelter of the rock, when Lord Ruthven received a shot in the shoulder, which brought him to the ground. Aubrey hastened to his assistance; and, no longer heeding the contest of his own peril, was soon surprised by seeing the robbers' faces around him – his guards having, upon Lord

Ruthven's being wounded, immediately thrown up their arms and surrendered.

By promises of great reward, Aubrey soon induced them to convey his wounded friend to a neighbouring cabin; and having agreed upon a ransom, he was no more disturbed by their presence – they being content merely to guard the entrance till their comrade should return with the promised sum, for which he had an order. Lord Ruthven's strength rapidly decreased; in two days mortification ensued, and death seemed advancing with hasty steps. His conduct and appearance had not changed; he seemed as unconscious of pain as he had been of the objects about him: but towards the close of the last evening, his mind became apparently uneasy, and his eye often fixed upon Aubrey, who was induced to offer his assistance with more than usual earnestness – 'Assist me! you may save me – you may do more than that – I mean not my life, I heed the death of my existence as little as that of the passing day; but you may save my honour, your friend's honour.' 'How? tell me how? I would do anything,' replied Aubrey. 'I need but little – my life ebbs apace – I cannot explain the whole – but if you would conceal all you know of me, my honour were free from stain in the world's mouth – and if my death were unknown for some time in England – I – I – but life.' 'It shall not be known.' 'Swear!' cried the dying man, raising himself with exultant violence, 'Swear by all your soul reveres, by all your nature fears, swear that for a year and a day you will not impart your knowledge of my crimes or death to any living being in any way, whatever may happen, or whatever you may see.' His eyes seemed bursting from their sockets: 'I swear!' said Aubrey; he sunk laughing upon his pillow, and breathed no more.

Aubrey retired to rest, but did not sleep; the many circumstances attending his acquaintance with this man rose upon his mind, and he knew not why; when he remembered his oath a cold shivering came over him, as if from the presentiment of something horrible awaiting him. Rising early in the morning, he was about to enter the hovel in which he had left the corpse, when a robber met him, and informed him that it was no longer there, having been conveyed by himself and comrades, upon his retiring, to the pinnacle of a neighbouring mount, according to a promise they had given his lordship, that it should be exposed to the first cold ray of the moon that rose after his death. Aubrey was astonished, and taking several of the men, determined to go and bury it upon the spot where it lay. But, when he had mounted to the summit he found no trace of either the corpse or the clothes, though the robbers swore they pointed out the identical rock on which they had laid the body. For a time his mind was bewildered in conjectures, but he at last returned, convinced that they had buried the corpse for the sake of the clothes.

Weary of a country in which he had met with such terrible misfortunes, and in which all apparently conspired to heighten that superstitious melancholy that had seized upon his mind, he resolved to leave it, and soon arrived at Smyrna. While waiting for a vessel to convey him to Otranto, or to Naples, he occupied himself in arranging those effects he had with him belonging to Lord Ruthven. Amongst other things there was a case containing several weapons of offence, more or less adapted to ensure the death of the victim. There were several daggers and ataghans. Whilst turning them over, and examining their curious forms, what was his surprise at finding a sheath apparently ornamented in the same style as the dagger discovered in the fatal hut – he shuddered – hastening to gain further proof, he found the weapon, and his horror may be imagined when he discovered that it fitted, though peculiarly shaped, the sheath he held in his hand. His eyes seemed to need no further certainty – they seemed gazing to be bound to the dagger; yet still he wished to disbelieve; but the particular form, the same varying tints upon the haft and sheath were alike in splendour on both, and left no room for doubt; there were also drops of blood on each.

He left Smyrna, and on his way home, at Rome, his first inquiries were concerning the lady he had attempted to snatch from Lord Ruthven's seductive arts. Her parents were in distress, their fortune ruined, and she had not been heard of since the departure of his lordship. Aubrey's mind became almost broken under so many repeated horrors; he was afraid that this lady had fallen a victim to the destroyer of Ianthe. He became morose and silent; and his only occupation consisted in urging the speed of the postilions, as if he were going to save the life of someone he held dear. He arrived at Calais; a breeze, which seemed obedient to his will, soon wafted him to the English shores; and he hastened to the mansion of his fathers, and there, for a moment, appeared to lose, in the embraces and caresses of his sister, all memory of the past. If she before, by her infantine caresses, had gained his affection, now that the woman began to appear, she was still more attaching as a companion.

Miss Aubrey had not that winning grace which gains the gaze and applause of the drawing-room assemblies. There was none of that light brilliancy which only exists in the heated atmosphere of a crowded apartment. Her blue eye was never lit up by the levity of the mind beneath. There was a melancholy charm about it which did not seem to arise from misfortune, but from some feeling within, that appeared to indicate a soul conscious of a brighter realm. Her step was not that light footing, which strays where'er a butterfly or a colour may attract – it was sedate and pensive. When alone, her face was never brightened by the smile of joy; but when her brother breathed to her his affection, and would in her presence forget those griefs she knew destroyed his rest, who would have exchanged her smile for that of the voluptuary? It seemed as if those eyes, that face were then playing in the light of their own native sphere. She was yet only eighteen, and had not been presented to the world, it having been thought by her guardians more fit that her presentation should be delayed until her brother's return from the continent, when he might be her protector. It was now, therefore, resolved that the next drawing-room, which was fast approaching, should be the epoch of her entry into the 'busy scene'. Aubrey would rather have remained in the mansion of his fathers, and fed upon the melancholy which overpowered him. He could not feel interest about the frivolities of fashionable strangers, when his mind had been so torn by the events he had witnessed; but he determined to sacrifice his own comfort to the protection of his sister. They soon arrived in town, and prepared for the next day, which had been announced as a drawing-room.

The crowd was excessive – a drawing-room had not been held for a long time, and all who were anxious to bask in the smile of royalty, hastened thither. Aubrey was there with his sister. While he was standing in a corner by himself, heedless of all around him, engaged in the remembrance that the first time he had seen Lord Ruthven was in that very place – he felt himself suddenly seized by the arm, and a voice he recognised too well, sounded in his ear – 'Remember your oath.' He had hardly courage to turn, fearful of seeing a spectre that would blast him, when he perceived, at a little distance, the same figure which had attracted his notice on this spot upon his first entry into society. He gazed till his limbs almost refusing to bear their weight, he was obliged to take the arm of a friend, and forcing a passage through the crowd, he threw himself into his carriage, and was driven home. He paced the room with hurried steps, and fixed his hands upon his head, as if he were afraid his thoughts were bursting from his brain. Lord Ruthven again before him – circumstances started up in dreadful array – the dagger – his oath. He roused himself, he could not believe it possible – the dead rise again! He thought his imagination had conjured up the image his mind was resting upon. It was impossible that it could be real – he determined, therefore, to go again into society; for though he attempted to ask concerning Lord Ruthven, the name hung upon his lips, and he could not succeed in gaining information. He went a few nights after with his sister to the assembly of a near relation. Leaving her under the protection of a matron, he retired into a recess, and there gave himself up to his own devouring thoughts. Perceiving, at last, that many were leaving, he roused himself, and entering another room, found his sister surrounded by several apparently in earnest conversation; he attempted to pass and get near her, when one, whom he requested to move, turned round, and revealed to him those features he most abhorred. He sprang forward, seized his sister's arm, and, with hurried step, forced her towards the street: at the door he found himself impeded by the crowd of servants who were waiting for their lords; and while he was engaged in passing them, he again heard that voice whisper close to him – 'Remember your oath!' He did not dare to turn, but, hurrying his sister, soon reached home.

Aubrey became almost distracted. If before his mind had been absorbed by one subject, how much more completely was it engrossed, now that the certainty of the monster's living again pressed upon his thoughts. His sister's attentions were now unheeded, and it was in vain that she entreated him to explain to her what had caused his abrupt conduct. He only uttered a few words, and those terrified her. The more he thought, the more he was bewildered. His oath startled him – was he then to allow this monster to roam, bearing ruin upon his breath, amidst all he held dear, and not avert its progress? His very sister might have been touched by him. But even if he were to break his oath, and disclose his suspicions, who would believe him? He thought of employing his own hand to free the world from such a wretch; but death, he remembered, had been already mocked. For days he remained in this state; shut up in his room, he saw no one, and ate only when his sister came, who, with eyes streaming with tears, besought him, for her sake, to support nature. At last, no longer capable of bearing stillness and solitude, he left his house, roamed from street to street, anxious to fly that image which haunted him. His dress became neglected, and he wandered, as often exposed to the noon-day sun as to the midnight damps. He was no longer to be recognised; at first he returned with the evening to the house; but at last he laid himself down to rest wherever fatigue overtook him. His sister, anxious for his safety, employed people to follow him; but they were soon distanced by him who fled from a pursuer swifter than any – from thought. His conduct, however, suddenly changed. Struck with the idea that he left by his absence the whole of his friends, with a fiend amongst them, of whose presence they were unconscious, he determined to enter again into society, and watch him closely, anxious to forewarn, in spite of his oath, all whom Lord Ruthven approached with intimacy. But when he entered into a room, his haggard and suspicious looks were so striking, his inward shudderings so visible, that his sister was at last obliged to beg of him to abstain from seeking, for her sake, a society which affected him so strongly. When, however, remonstrance proved unavailing, the guardians thought proper to interpose, and, fearing that his mind was becoming alienated, they thought it high time to resume again that trust which had been before imposed upon them by Aubrey's parents.

Desirous of saving him from the injuries and sufferings he had daily encountered in his wanderings, and of preventing him from exposing to the general eye those marks of what they considered folly, they engaged a physician to reside in the house, and take constant care of him. He hardly appeared to notice it, so completely was his mind absorbed by one terrible subject. His incoherence became at last so great, that he was confined to his chamber. There he would often lie for days, incapable of being roused. He had become emaciated, his eyes had attained a glassy lustre – the only sign of affection and recollection remaining displayed itself upon the entry of his sister; then he would sometimes start, and, seizing her hands, with looks that severely afflicted her, he would desire her not to touch him. 'Oh, do not touch him—if your love for me is aught, do not go near him!' When, however, she enquired to whom he referred, his only answer was, 'True! true!' and again he sank into a state, whence not even she could rouse him. This lasted many months: gradually, however, as the year was passing, his incoherences became less frequent, and his mind threw off a portion of its gloom, whilst his guardians observed, that several times in the day he would count upon his fingers a definite number, and then smile.

The time had nearly elapsed, when, upon the last day of the year, one of his guardians entering his room, began to converse with his physician upon the melancholy circumstance of Aubrey's being in so awful a situation, when his sister was going next day to be married. Instantly Aubrey's attention was at racted; he asked anxiously to whom. Glad of this mark of returning intellect, of which they feared he had been deprived, they mentioned the name of the Earl of Marsden. Thinking this was a young Earl whom he had met with in society, Aubrey seemed pleased, and astonished them still more by his expressing his intention to be present at the nuptials, and desiring to see his sister. They answered not, but in a few minutes his sister was with him. He was apparently again capable of being affected by the influence of her lovely smile; for he pressed her to his breast, and kissed her cheek, wet with tears, flowing at the thought of her brother's being once more alive to the feelings of affection. He began to speak with all his wonted warmth, and to congratulate her upon her marriage with a person so distinguished for rank and every accomplishment; when he suddenly perceived a locket upon her breast; opening it, what was his surprise at beholding the features of the monster who had so long influenced his life. He seized the portrait in a paroxysm of rage, and trampled it under foot. Upon her asking him why he thus destroyed the resemblance of her future husband, he looked as if he did not understand her – then seizing her hands, and gazing on her with a frantic expression of countenance, he bade her swear that she would never wed this monster, for he – But he could not advance – it seemed as if that voice again bade him remember his oath – he turned suddenly round, thinking Lord Ruthven was near him but saw no one. In the meantime the guardians and physician, who had heard the whole, and thought this was but a return of his disorder, entered, and forcing him from Miss Aubrey, desired her to leave him. He fell upon his knees to them, he implored, he begged of them to delay but one day. They, attributing this to the insanity they imagined had taken possession of his mind, endeavoured to pacify him, and retired.

Lord Ruthven had called the morning after the drawing-room, and had been refused with everyone else. When he heard of Aubrey's ill health, he readily understood himself to be the cause of it; but when he learned that he was deemed insane, his exultation and pleasure could hardly be concealed from those among whom he had gained this information. He hastened to the house of his former companion, and, by constant attendance, and the pretence of great affection for the brother and interest in his fate, he gradually won the ear of Miss Aubrey. Who could resist his power? His tongue had dangers and toils to recount – could speak of himself as of an individual having no sympathy with any being on the crowded earth, save with her to whom he addressed himself – could tell how, since he knew her, his existence had begun to seem worthy of preservation, if it were merely that he might listen to her soothing accents – in fine, he knew so well how to use the serpent's art, or such was the will of fate, that he gained her affections. The title of the elder branch falling at length to him, he obtained an important embassy, which served as an excuse for hastening the marriage (in spite of her brother's deranged state), which was to take place the very day before his departure for the continent.

Aubrey, when he was left by the physician and his guardians, attempted to bribe the servants, but in vain. He asked for pen and paper; it was given him; he wrote a letter to his sister, conjuring her, as she valued her own happiness, her own honour, and the honour of those now in the grave, who once held her in their arms as their hope and the hope of their house, to delay but for a few hours that marriage, on which he denounced the most heavy curses. The servants promised they would deliver it; but giving it to the physician, he thought it better not to harass any more the mind of Miss Aubrey by, what he considered, the ravings of a maniac. Night passed on without rest to the busy inmates of the house; and Aubrey heard, with a horror that may more easily be conceived than described, the notes of busy preparation. Morning came, and the sound of carriages broke upon his ear. Aubrey grew almost frantic. The curiosity of the servants at last overcame their vigilance, they gradually stole away, leaving him in the custody of a helpless old woman. He seized the opportunity, with one bound was out of the room, and in a moment found himself in the apartment where all were nearly assembled. Lord Ruthven was the first to perceive him: he immediately approached, and, taking his arm by force, hurried him from the room, speechless with rage. When on the staircase, Lord Ruthven whispered in his ear – 'Remember your oath, and know, if not my bride today, your sister is dishonoured. Women are frail!' So saying, he pushed him towards his attendants, who, roused by the old woman, had come in search of him. Aubrey could no longer support himself; his rage not finding vent, had broken a blood-vessel, and he was conveyed to bed. This was not mentioned to his sister, who was not present when he entered, as the physician was afraid of agitating her. The marriage was solemnised, and the bride and bridegroom left London.

Aubrey's weakness increased; the effusion of blood produced symptoms of the near approach of death. He desired his sister's guardians might be called, and when the midnight hour had struck, he related composedly what the reader has perused – he died immediately after.

The guardians hastened to protect Miss Aubrey; but when they arrived, it was too late. Lord Ruthven had disappeared, and Aubrey's sister had glutted the thirst of a VAMPYRE!

A Werewolf of the Campagna

MRS HUGH FRASER

Santiago is rich in gruesome things, but the most terrifying that I ever saw there was when I was leaning out of the drawing-room window one night, just before I went to bed. It was late, and there was a bright moon shining that threw the whole of the Alameda into vivid relief. I had been absorbed in my thoughts for some time, trying to dream myself back into Italy, and see, in the stucco *palatios*, the real palaces of Rome – wondering what all the dear people there were doing (one has to snatch at the tricks of childhood sometimes in the ends of the earth, to help quiet the *Heimweh*), when, suddenly, from far up the street, I heard the howl of a wolf. There was no mistaking it. It was not a dog; no dog had ever lived that could imitate it. Staring down in the direction from which it came, I saw the figure of a man lurch out of the trees into the full light of the moon – a man dressed in evening clothes – I could see the white shirt-front clearly. On he came, staggering from side to side, and bumping his head crazily against the trees, as though trying to break them down – and not by accident, for I saw him, three or four times, lower his head and run at them. And all the time he howled – that awful howl of a wolf!

The street was quite deserted, not even a policeman being in sight, and I had a full view of him as he passed beneath the window. His eyes were shut, his lips were drawn back in a grin that showed his teeth, and his mouth was wide open. I could not leave the window, though my own teeth were chattering like castanets, and I was trembling all over. Down the street I watched him go, weaving from side to side in the moonlight, and rushing, head-on, against the trees, howling, until at last he disappeared in the distance. But the screeching came back to me for two or three minutes after he had vanished himself.

What was it? The good God who made him only knows. He was not drunk, for no drunken man could have thrown himself at the trees in that fashion – and no sober man, either, that I have ever seen

103

or heard of. The howl, at least, was not that of any human being, whatever the body might have been. It was that of a famished wolf and not anything else. Does that sound like superstition? Well, superstition it may be. But which is the worst offender – he who, having seen much and experienced many strange adventures, prefers to think all things possible in the creation of an omnipotent God, or he who fastens that word 'superstition' over the entrance to every avenue of knowledge that pertains to the Twilight Kingdom?

I am reminded of an article I read some time ago on the subject of miracles by a divine of one of the free churches, whose name I forget. Having set forth his belief in an almighty and all-powerful Providence, the writer set himself the task of attempting to prove the miracles could not happen in our day – and this is how he went about it. Compelled by the incontrovertible evidence of the Gospel, he acknowledged that our Lord performed many in His time, and that His followers performed many more. But, he went on to say, such things then were obviously needed to convert the heathen and give the church a start. Leaving it to be understood that no such necessity existed nowadays, there being, presumably, no more heathen to convert, he let fall the astounding observation that, should an all-just, all-seeing, all-understanding God, in His infinite wisdom, do such a thing in our time – and fly in the face of the writer's personal opinions on the subject – he would cease ('cease!' the Eternal would 'cease!' that was his word) to be a just God, thereby, of course, ceasing to be God at all! Put into plainer words, the Almighty might continue to sit on His throne as long as He behaved Himself in accordance with the reverend gentleman's idea of how a God should behave – but not a moment longer. And the writer was – will you believe it? – a Professor of Theology at a nonconformist seminary!

It is a strange attitude of mind that acknowledges omnipotence in one breath and sets rigid limits to it in the next. But to go back to the man-wolf.

One of our old Italian servants used to tell a fearful story – and she spoke of it as though it were of common knowledge. It was about a certain hunter who lived far out in the Campagna by himself, in a small stone house. One evening, just as he was preparing to go to bed, he heard someone knocking at the door and, opening it, saw a man and a woman of the better class standing outside. They were well dressed, although the woman was dusty and tired, and they begged him to let them stay the night, the man saying that they had gone for a walk earlier in the day, taking some food with them, and intending to return to Rome in the evening. After eating, he had taken a little nap, and when he woke up, found that his wife had disappeared. She had wandered away to pick some flowers, from her own account, and had lost herself – a simple enough thing to do thereabouts. They were ready to pay handsomely, they said, for the night's lodging, and he, glad enough to earn money so easily, led them in and, having given them something to eat and drink, led them upstairs and left them there. The next morning, as he was leaving the house, the husband called out to him that he would be very glad to buy from him any game that he might get, and added that he was going back to bed again – for he was singularly sleepy.

The man started off – cheerfully, as one may understand – and the other went back to bed, where he slept until the early afternoon. On awakening, he saw that his wife was sitting by one of the windows, wrapped in a shawl. She was cold, she said, and anxious to start for home again as soon as possible. He assured her that he would not keep her waiting for long, dressed himself, and went downstairs, leaving her by the window.

Having refreshed himself, he sat down by the door, borrowing his host's pipe and tobacco, and waited for the latter's return. After some time had sped he left the house and walked a little way in the direction which the hunter had taken in the morning, but he had not proceeded far before he met him. The man was evidently labouring under some great excitement, and he also seemed to be very dizzy, for he staggered as he came up, and sat down abruptly. His game-bag was empty, but the other noticed a smear of blood on his coat, and, thinking him to have met with some accident, stooped down. But the hunter waved him back. He could not speak for a minute or two, and only after he had recovered himself somewhat he told his story.

A mile or so from the house he had sat down to rest and look about for the signs of any game. The day was very still, and he had been listening and watching intently, when, without an instant's warning, a heavy body leaped on him from behind, threw him over, and held him in a pair of mighty jaws by the coat-collar, face downward. So stunned was he with fright and astonishment that, at first, he lay still. But presently, as the teeth began to work upwards towards his neck he wriggled his head around and saw, a few inches away, the paw of an enormous wolf. Wolves there were, as he said, and wolves, but nothing like this one had he ever heard of. In proof of which, he showed the barrel of his gun which had been slung on his back, bitten almost in two. His hands had been free, and he had managed to get out his knife, hardly knowing what to do with it, till his eyes fell once more on the great paw by his head. In desperation, he slashed at it, and the long, razor-edged blade went through bone and flesh; when, with a howl, the wolf jumped away from him, and he fainted.

How long he lay there he had no idea, but when he came to himself, and got to his feet, the paw was beside him. So saying, he produced it – and it bore out his story, for it was larger than a man's hand. Together they returned to the house, where, after making sure that the hunter was none the worse for his experience, the visitor asked if he might look at the paw again. In the hasty glance he had had of it by the side of the road, he had not had time to satisfy his curiosity. Such a thing was not to be seen twice in a lifetime. The hunter agreed with him, and put his hand into his leather game-bag – only to withdraw it with a scream. 'Do not go near it!' he begged as the other approached. 'As you value your soul, do not touch it!'

But the visitor was made of sterner stuff, and, despite his host's pleadings, dived into the game-bag and brought out – a human hand!

Dropping it on the floor, he sprang away, but his eyes were drawn back to the gruesome thing in spite of him, and he saw the glitter of a ring. There was something diabolically familiar about the hand. He looked again and closer. There was something familiar about the ring, too. He had seen it elsewhere and very lately. He left his host in the chair where he had collapsed, ran upstairs, and burst in on his wife. She was still sitting by the window, and when she heard his voice she turned and looked at him. Her face was changed almost out of recognition, and the hate of the other world was in her eyes, but he seized the shawl she had wrapped around her, though she bit and struggled. At last he tore it off, and a glance showed him the rough bandages over one arm where the hand should have been. It was her hand that he had taken out of the game-bag! The end of the story (which I can only tell as it was told to me) is that the woman was burnt as a witch.

THE DOOMED SISTERS

Charles Robert Maturin

The tranquillity of the Catholics of Ireland during the disturbed periods of 1715 and 1745 was most commendable, and somewhat extraordinary; to enter into an analysis of their probable motives is not at all the object of the writer of this tale, as it is pleasanter to state the fact of their honour than at this distance of time to assign dubious and unsatisfactory reasons for it. Many of them, however, showed a kind of secret disgust at the existing state of affairs, by quitting their family residences and wandering about like persons who were uncertain of their homes, or possibly expecting better from some near and fortunate contingency.

Among the rest was a Jacobite Baronet who, sick of his uncongenial situation in a Whig neighbourhood, in the north—where he heard of nothing but the heroic defence of Londonderry; the barbarities of the French generals; and the resistless exhortations of the godly Mr Walker, a Presbyterian clergyman to whom the citizens gave the title of 'Evangelist';—quitted his paternal residence, and about the year 1720 hired the Castle of Leixlip for three years (it was then the property of the Conollys, who let it to triennial tenants); and removed thither with his family, which consisted of three daughters—their mother having long been dead.

The Castle of Leixlip, at that period, possessed a character of romantic beauty and feudal grandeur, such as few buildings in Ireland can claim, and which is now, alas, totally effaced by the destruction of its noble woods; on the destroyers of which the writer would wish 'a minstrel's malison were said'. Leixlip, though about seven miles from Dublin, has all the sequestered and picturesque character that imagination could ascribe to a landscape a hundred miles from, not only the metropolis but an inhabited town. After driving a dull mile (an *Irish* mile) in passing from Lucan to Leixlip, the road—hedged up on one side of the high wall that bounds the demesne of the Veseys, and on the other by low enclosures, over whose rugged tops you have no view at all— at once opens on Leixlip Bridge, at almost a right angle, and displays a luxury of landscape on which the eye that has seen it even in childhood dwells with delighted recollection. Leixlip Bridge, a rude but solid structure, projects from a high bank of the Liffey, and slopes rapidly to the opposite side, which there lies remarkably low. To the right the plantations of the Veseys' demesne—no longer obscured by walls—almost mingle their dark woods in its stream, with the opposite ones of Marshfield and St Catharine's. The river is scarcely visible, overshadowed as it is by the deep, rich and bending foliage of the trees. To the left it bursts out in all the brilliancy of light, washes the garden steps of the houses of Leixlip, wanders round the low walls of its church-yard, plays with the pleasure-boat moored under the arches on which the summer-house of the Castle is raised, and then loses itself among the rich woods that once skirted those grounds to its very brink. The contrast on the other side, with the luxuriant vegetation, the lighter and more diversified arrangement of ter-raced walks, scattered shrubberies, temples seated on pinnacles, and thickets that conceal from you the sight of the river until you are on its banks, that mark the character of the grounds which are now the property of Colonel Marley, is peculiarly striking.

Visible above the highest roofs of the town, though a quarter of a mile distant from them, are the ruins of Confy Castle, a right good old predatory tower of the stirring times when blood was shed like water; and as you pass the bridge you catch a glimpse of the waterfall (or salmon-leap, as it is called) on whose noon-day lustre, or moonlight beauty, probably the rough livers of that age when Confy Castle was 'a tower of strength', never glanced an eye or cast a thought as they clattered in their harness over Leixlip Bridge, or waded through the stream before that convenience was in existence.

Whether the solitude in which he lived contributed to tranquil-lise Sir Redmond Blaney's feelings, or whether they had begun to rust from want of collision with those of others, it is impossible to say, but certain it is that the good Baronet began gradually to lose his tenacity in political matters; and except when a Jacobite friend came to dine with him, and drink with many a significant 'nod and beck and smile, the King over the water—or the parish priest (good man) spoke of the hopes of better times, and the final suc-cess of the *right* cause, and the old religion—or a Jacobite servant was heard in the solitude of the large mansion whistling 'Charlie is my darling', to which Sir Redmond involuntarily responded in a deep bass voice, somewhat the worse for wear, and marked with more emphasis than good discretion—except, as I have said, on such occasions, the Baronet's politics, like his life, seemed passing away without notice or effort. Domestic calamities, too, pressed sorely on the old gentleman: of his three daughters, the youngest, Jane, had disappeared in so extraordinary a manner in her child-hood, that though it is but a wild, remote family tradition, I cannot help relating it.

The girl was of uncommon beauty and intelligence, and was suffered to wander about the neighbourhood of the castle with the daughter of a servant, who was also called Jane, as a *nom de caresse*. One evening Jane Blaney and her young companion went far and deep into the woods; their absence created no uneasiness at the time, as these excursions were by no means unusual, till her playfellow returned home alone and weeping, at a very late hour. Her account was that, in passing through a lane at some distance from the castle, an old woman, in the *Fingallian* dress (a red petticoat and a long green jacket), suddenly started out of a thicket, and took Jane Blaney by the arm: she had in her hand two rushes, one of which she threw over her shoulder, and giving the other to the child, motioned to her to do the same. Her young companion, terrified at what she saw, was running away, when Jane Blaney called after her—'Good-bye, good-bye, it is a long time before you will see me again.' The girl said they then dis-appeared, and she found her way home as she could. An inde-fatigable search was immediately commenced—woods were traversed, thickets were explored, ponds were drained—all in vain. The pursuit and the hope were at length given up. Ten years afterwards, the housekeeper of Sir Redmond, having remembered that she left the key of a closet where sweetmeats were kept on the kitchen-table, returned to fetch it. As she approached the door, she heard a childish voice murmuring—'Cold—cold—cold how long it is since I have felt a fire!' She advanced, and saw, to her amazement, Jane Blaney, shrunk to half her usual size, and covered with rags, crouching over the embers of the fire. The housekeeper flew in terror from the spot, and roused the servants, but the vision had fled. The child was reported to have been seen several times afterwards, as diminutive in form as though she had not grown an inch since she was ten years of age, and always crouching over a fire, whether in the turret-room or kitchen, complaining of cold and hunger, and apparently covered with rags. Her existence is still said to be protracted under these dismal circumstances, so unlike those of Lucy Gray in Wordsworth's beautiful ballad:

> Yet some will say, that to this day
>   She is a living child—
> That they have met sweet Lucy Gray
>   Upon the lonely wild;
> O'er rough and smooth she trips along,
>   And never looks behind;
> And hums a solitary song
>   That whistles in the wind.

The fate of the eldest daughter was more melancholy, though less extraordinary; she was addressed by a gentleman of competent fortune and unexceptionable character: he was a Catholic, moreover; and Sir Redmond Blaney signed the marriage articles, in full satisfaction of the security of his daughter's soul, as well as of her jointure. The marriage was celebrated at the Castle of Leixlip; and, after the bride and bridegroom had retired, the guests still remained drinking to their future happiness when suddenly, to the great alarm of Sir Redmond and his friends, loud and piercing cries were heard to issue from the part of the castle in which the bridal chamber was situated.

Some of the more courageous hurried upstairs; it was too late— the wretched bridegroom had burst, on that fatal night, into a sudden and most horrible paroxysm of insanity. The mangled form of the unfortunate and expiring lady bore attestation to the mortal virulence with which the disease had operated on the wretched husband, and died a victim to it himself after the involuntary murder of his bride. The bodies were interred, as soon as decency would permit, and the story hushed up.

Sir Redmond's hopes of Jane's recovery were diminishing every day, though he still continued to listen to every wild tale told by the domestics; and all his care was supposed to be now directed towards his only surviving daughter. Anne, living in solitude, and partaking only of the very limited education of Irish females of that period, was left very much to the servants, among whom she increased her taste for superstitious and supernatural horrors, to a degree that had a most disastrous effect on her future life.

Among the numerous menials of the Castle there was one 'withered crone' who had been nurse to the late Lady Blaney's mother, and whose memory was a complete *Thesaurus terrorum*. The mysterious fate of Jane first encouraged her sister to listen to the wild tales of this hag, who avouched that at one time she saw the fugitive standing before the portrait of her late mother in one of the apartments of the Castle, and muttering to herself—'Woe's me, woe's me! how little my mother thought her wee Jane would ever come to be what she is!' But as Anne grew older she began more 'seriously to incline' to the hag's promises that she could show her her future bridegroom, on the performance of certain ceremonies which she at first revolted from as horrible and impious; but, finally, at the repeated instigation of the old woman, consented to act a part in. The period fixed upon for the performance of these unhallowed rites was now approaching—it was near the 31st of October, the eventful night when such ceremonies were, and still are supposed, in the North of Ireland, to be most potent in their effects. All day long the Crone took care to lower the mind of the young lady to the proper key of submissive and trembling credulity, by every horrible story she could relate; and she told them with frightful and supernatural energy. This woman was called *Collogue* by the family, a name equivalent to Gossip in England, or Cummer in Scotland (though her real name was Bridget Dease); and she verified the name by the exercise of an unwearied loquacity, an indefatigable memory, and a rage for communicating and inflicting terror that spared no victim in the household, from the groom, whom she sent shivering to his rug, to the Lady of the Castle, over whom she felt she held unbounded sway.

The 31st of October arrived—the Castle was perfectly quiet before eleven o'clock; half an hour afterwards, the Collogue and Anne Blaney were seen gliding along a passage that led to what is called King John's Tower, where it is said that monarch received the homage of the Irish princes as Lord of Ireland, and which, at all events, is the most ancient part of the structure. The Collogue opened a small door with a key which she had secreted about her, and urged the young lady to hurry on. Anne advanced to the postern, and stood there irresolute and trembling like a timid swimmer on the bank of an unknown stream. It was a dark autumnal evening; a heavy wind sighed among the woods of the Castle, and bowed the branches of the lower trees almost to the waves of the Liffey which, swelled by recent rains, struggled and roared amid the stones that obstructed its channel. The steep descent from the Castle lay before her, with its dark avenue of elms; a few lights still burned in the little village of Leixlip—but from the lateness of the hour it was probable they would soon be extinguished.

The lady lingered. 'And must I go alone?' said she, foreseeing that the terrors of her fearful journey could be aggravated by her more fearful purpose.

'Ye must, or all will be spoiled,' said the hag, shading the miserable light, that did not extend its influence above six inches on the path of the victim. 'Ye must go alone—and I will watch for you here, dear, till you come back, and then see what will come to you at twelve o'clock.'

The unfortunate girl paused. 'Oh! Collogue, Collogue, if you would but come with me. Oh! Collogue, come with me, if it be but to the bottom of the castle-hill.'

'If I went with you, dear, we should never reach the top of it alive again, for there are them near that would tear us both in pieces.'

'Oh! Collogue, Collogue—let me turn back then, and go to my own room—I have advanced too far, and I have done too much.'

'And that's what you have, dear, and so you must go further, and do more still, unless, when you return to your own room, you would see the likeness of *some one* instead of a handsome young bridegroom.'

The young lady looked about her for a moment, terror and wild hope trembling at her heart—then, with a sudden impulse of supernatural courage, she darted like a bird from the terrace of the Castle, the fluttering of her white garments was seen for a few moments, and then the hag who had been shading the flickering light with her hand, bolted the postern and, placing the candle before a glazed loophole, sat down on a stone seat in the recess of the tower, to watch the event of the spell. It was an hour before the young lady returned; when her face was as pale, and her eyes as fixed, as those of a dead body, but she held in her grasp *a dripping garment*, a proof that her errand had been performed. She flung it into her companion's hands, and then stood panting and gazing wildly about her as if she knew not where she was. The hag herself grew terrified at the insane and breathless state of her victim, and hurried her to her chamber; but here the preparations for the terrible ceremonies of the night were the first objects that struck her and, shivering at the sight, she covered her eyes with her hands, and stood immovably fixed in the middle of the room.

It needed all the hag's persuasions (aided even by mysterious menaces), combined with the returning faculties and reviving curiosity of the poor girl, to prevail on her to go through the remaining business of the night. At length she said, as if in desperation, 'I *will* go through with it: but be in the next room; and if what I dread should happen, I will ring my father's little silver bell which I have secured for the night—and as you have a soul to be saved, Collogue, come to me at its very first sound.'

The hag promised, gave her last instructions with eager and jealous minuteness, and then retired to her own room, which was adjacent to that of the young lady. Her candle had burned out, but she stirred up the embers of her turf fire, and sat nodding over them, and smoothing her pallet from time to time, but resolved not to lie down while there was a chance of a sound from the lady's room, for which she herself, withered as her feelings were, waited with a mingled feeling of anxiety and terror.

It was now long past midnight, and all was silent as the grave throughout the Castle. The hag dozed over the embers till her head touched her knees, then started up as the sound of the bell seemed to tinkle in her ears, then dozed again, and again started as the bell appeared to tinkle more distinctly—suddenly she was roused, not by the bell, but by the most piercing and horrible cries from the neighbouring chamber. The Crone, aghast for the first time at the possible consequences of the mischief she might have occasioned, hastened to the room. Anne was in convulsions, and the hag was compelled reluctantly to call up the housekeeper (removing meanwhile the implements of the ceremony), and assist in applying all the specifics known at that day, burnt feathers, etc., to restore her. When they had at length succeeded, the house-keeper was dismissed, the door was bolted, and the Collogue was left alone with Anne; the subject of their conference might have been guessed at, but was not known until many years afterwards; but Anne that night held in her hand, in the shape of a weapon with the use of which neither of them was acquainted, an evidence that her chamber had been visited by a being of no earthly form.

This evidence the hag importuned her to destroy, or to remove, but she persisted with fatal tenacity in keeping it. She locked it up, however, immediately, and seemed to think she had acquired a right, since she had grappled so fearfully with the mysteries of futurity, to know all the secrets of which that weapon might yet lead to the disclosure. But from that night it was observed that her character, her manner, and even her countenance, became altered. She grew stern and solitary, shrank at the sight of her former associates, and imperatively forbade the slightest allusion to the circumstances which had occasioned this mysterious change.

It was a few days subsequent to this event that Anne, who after dinner had left the Chaplain reading the life of St Francis Xavier to Sir Redmond, and retired to her own room to work and, per-haps, to muse, was surprised to hear the bell at the outer gate ring loudly and repeatedly—a sound she had never heard since her first residence in the Castle; for the few guests who resorted there came and departed as noiselessly as humble visitors at the house of a great man generally do. Straight way there rode up the avenue of elms, which we have already mentioned, a stately gentleman, followed by four servants, all mounted, the two former having pistols in their holsters, and the two latter carrying saddle-bags before them: though it was the first week in November, the dinner hour being one o'clock, Anne had light enough to notice all these circumstances. The arrival of the stranger seemed to cause much, though not unwelcome tumult in the Castle; orders were loudly and hastily given for the accommodation of the servants and horses—steps were heard traversing the numerous passages for a full hour—then all was still; and it was said that Sir Redmond had locked with his own hand the door of the room where he and the stranger sat, and desired that no one should dare to approach it. About two hours afterwards, a female servant came with orders from her master to have a plentiful supper ready by eight o'clock, at which he desired the presence of his daughter. The family establishment was on a handsome scale for an Irish house, and Anne had only to descend to the kitchen to order the roasted chickens to be well strewed with brown sugar according to the unrefined fashion of the day, to inspect the mixing of a bowl of sago with its allowance of a bottle of port wine and a large handful of the richest spices, and to order particularly that the pease pudding should have a huge lump of cold salt butter stuck in its centre; and then, her household cares being over, to retire to her room and array herself in a robe of white damask for the occasion. At eight o'clock she was summoned to the supper-room. She came in, according to the fashion of the times, with the first dish; but as she passed through the ante-room, where the servants were holding lights and bearing the dishes, her sleeve was twitched, and the ghastly face of the Collogue pushed close to hers; while she muttered 'Did not I say *he would come for you*, dear?' Anne's blood ran cold, but she advanced, saluted her father and the stranger with two low and distinct reverences, and then took her place at the table. Her feelings of awe and perhaps terror at the whisper of her associate were not diminished by the appearance of the stranger; there was a singular and mute solemnity in his manner during the meal. He ate nothing. Sir Redmond appeared constrained, gloomy and thoughtful. At length, starting, he said (without naming the stranger's name), 'You will drink my daughter's health?' The stranger intimated his willingness to have that honour, but absently filled his glass with water; Anne put a few drops of wine into hers, and bowed towards him. At that moment, for the first time since they had met, she beheld his face—it was pale as that of a corpse. The deadly whiteness of his cheeks and lips, the hollow and distant sound of his voice, and the strange lustre of his large, dark, moveless eyes, strongly fixed on her, made her pause and even tremble as she raised the glass to her lips; she set it down, and the with another silent reverence retired to her chamber.

There she found Bridget Dease, busy in collecting the turf that burned on the hearth, for there was no grate in the apartment. 'Why are you here?' she said, impatiently.

The hag turned on her, with a ghastly grin of congratulation. 'Did not I tell you that *he* would come for you?'

'I believe he has,' said the unfortunate girl, sinking into the huge wicker chair by her bedside; 'for never did I see mortal with such a look.'

'But is not he a fine stately gentleman?' pursued the hag.

'He looks as if he were not of this world,' said Anne.

'Of this world, or of the next,' said the hag, raising her bony forefinger, 'mark my words – so sure as the (here she repeated some of the horrible formularies of the 31st of October) so sure he will be your bridegroom.'

'Then I shall be the bride of a corpse,' said Anne; 'for he I saw tonight is no living man.'

A fortnight elapsed, and whether Anne became reconciled to the features she had thought so ghastly, by the discovery that they were the handsomest she had ever beheld—and that the voice, whose sound at first was so strange and unearthly, was subdued into a tone of plaintive softness when addressing her—or whether it is impossible for two young persons with unoccupied hearts to meet in the country, and meet often, to gaze silently on the same stream, wander under the same trees, and listen together to the wind that waves the branches, without experiencing an assimilation of feeling rapidly succeeding an assimilation of taste; or whether it was from all these causes combined, but in less than a month Anne heard the declaration of the stranger's passion with many a blush, though without a sigh. He now avowed his name and rank. He stated himself to be a Scottish Baronet, of the name of Sir Richard Maxwell; family misfortunes had driven him from his country, and for ever precluded the possibility of his return: he had transferred his property to Ireland, and purposed to fix his residence there for life. Such was his statement. The courtship of those days was brief and simple. Anne became the wife of Sir Richard, and, I believe, they resided with her father till his death, when they removed to their estate in the North. There they remained for several years, in tranquillity and happiness, and had a numerous family. Sir Richard's conduct was marked by but two peculiarities: he not only shunned the intercourse, but the sight of any of his countrymen, and, if he happened to hear that a Scotsman had arrived in the neighbouring town, he shut himself up till assured of the stranger's departure. The other was his custom of retiring to his own chamber, and remaining invisible to his family on the anniversary of the 30th of October. The lady, who had her own associations connected with that period, only questioned him once on the subject of this seclusion, and was then solemnly and even sternly enjoined never to repeat her inquiry.

Matters stood thus, somewhat mysteriously, but not unhappily, when on a sudden, without any cause assigned or assignable, Sir Richard and Lady Maxwell parted, and never more met in this world, nor was she ever permitted to see one of her children to her dying hour. He continued to live at the family mansion, and she fixed her residence with a distant relative in a remote part of the country. So total was the disunion, that the name of either was never heard to pass the other's lips, from the moment of separation until that of dissolution.

Lady Maxwell survived Sir Richard forty years, living to the great age of 96; and, according to a promise, previously given, disclosed to a descendant with whom she had lived, the following extraordinary circumstances.

She said that on the night of the 30th of October, about seventy-five years before, at the instigation of her ill-advising attendant, she had washed one of her garments in a place where four streams met, and performed other unhallowed ceremonies under the direction of the Collogue, in the expectation that her future husband would appear to her in her chamber at twelve o'clock that night. The critical moment arrived, but with it no lover-like form. A vision of indescribable horror approached her bed, and flinging at her an iron weapon of a shape and construction unknown to her, bade her 'recognise her future husband by *that*.' The terrors of this visit soon deprived her of her senses; but on her recovery, she persisted, as has been said, in keeping the fearful pledge of the reality of the vision which, on examination, appeared to be incrusted with blood. It remained concealed in the inmost drawer of her cabinet till the morning of her separation. On that morning, Sir Richard Maxwell rose before daylight to join a hunting party. He wanted a knife for some accidental purpose and, missing his own, called to Lady Maxwell, who was still in bed, to lend him one. The lady, who was half asleep, answered, that in such a drawer of her cabinet he would find one. He went, however, to another, and the next moment she was fully awakened by seeing her husband present the terrible weapon to her throat, and threaten her with instant death unless she disclosed how she came by it. She supplicated for life, and then, in an agony of horror and contrition, told the tale of that eventful night. He gazed at her for a moment with a countenance which rage, hatred, and despair converted, as she avowed, into a living likeness of the demon-visage she had once beheld (so singularly was the fated resemblance fulfilled), and then exclaiming, 'You won me by the devil's aid, but you shall not keep me long,' left her—to meet no more in this world. Her husband's secret was not unknown to the lady, though the means by which she became possessed of it were wholly unwarrantable. Her curiosity had been strongly excited by her husband's aversion to his countrymen, and it was so stimulated by the arrival of a Scottish gentleman in the neighbourhood some time before, who professed himself formerly acquainted with Sir Richard, and spoke mysteriously of the causes that drove him from his country, that she contrived to procure an interview with him under a feigned name, and obtained from him the knowledge of circumstances which embittered her after-life to its latest hour. His story was this:

Sir Richard Maxwell was at deadly feud with a younger brother; a family feast was proposed to reconcile them, and as the use of knives and forks was then unknown in the Highlands, the company met armed with their dirks for the purpose of carving. They drank deeply; the feast, instead of harmonising, began to inflame their spirits; the topics of old strife were renewed; hands, that at first touched their weapons in defiance, drew them at last in fury, and in the fray, Sir Richard mortally wounded his brother. His life was with difficulty saved from the vengeance of the clan, and he was hurried towards the sea-coast, near which the house stood, and concealed there till a vessel could be procured to convey him to Ireland. He embarked *on the night of the 30th of October*, and while he was traversing the deck in unutterable agony of spirit, his hand accidentally touched the dirk which he had unconsciously worn ever since the fatal night. He drew it, and, praying 'that the guilt of his brother's blood might be as far from his soul as he could fling that weapon from his body', sent it with all his strength into the air. This instrument he found secreted in the lady's cabinet, and whether he really believed her to have become possessed of it by supernatural means, or whether he feared his wife was a secret witness of his crime, has not been ascertained, but the result was what I have stated.

The reparation took place on the discovery: for the rest,

> I know not how the truth may be,
> I tell the Tale as 'twas told to me.

THE HELL-FIRE CLUBS

Montague Summers

＊

Throughout the eighteenth century, in spite of the superficial and surface materialism, occult practices and the darker superstitions were rampant amongst all classes of society. More often than not the debauchery of the bucks and bloods, the Mohocks and the Sons of Midnight, the Blasters and Bumpers and Banditti, was demoniacal in the highest degree, their convivial meetings hardly to be distinguished from a sabbat orgy.

There were supernaturalistic impostors of every sort and kind – visionaries, mock mystics, pseudo-prophets, semi-sorcerers, 'white' witches, figure-casters, horoscopers, magnetizers, quack healers, convulsionaries, fortune-tellers, canting astrologers, initiates, sibyllas – in fact London and the whole countryside seethed with the cheats and corruptions of these Katerfeltos and Saganas.

The diabolical Societies in which the young Whig lords banded themselves together for the worship of Satan amid every circumstance of profligacy and blasphemy were generically known as 'hell-fire clubs'. As early as the reign of Queen Anne (1710) Ned Ward tells us that such a club forgathered at a vile tavern in Westminster. By 1721 these abominations had grown to such a height that King George I, by an Order in Council, commanded that instant action should be taken for the suppression of these 'horrid Impieties'. The members of these clubs meet, said the *Gazette*, 29 April, 1721, 'and in the most impious and blasphemous Manner, insult the most sacred Principles of our Holy Religion, affront Almighty God Himself', wherefore the King was 'resolved to make use of all the Authority committed to him by Almighty God, to punish such enormous Offenders, and to crush such shocking Impieties before they increase and draw down the Vengeance of God upon this Nation'. Further discoveries were made. Forty persons belonged to the Hell-Fire Club, which had various rendezvous at Somerset House, in the Strand, at a house in Westminster, and at another house in the fashionable Conduit Street, near Hanover Square. A broadside entitled *A Further and Particular Account of the Hell-Fire Sulphur-Society Clubs* supplies the most shocking details. The President was dubbed King of Hell, and it was common knowledge that the President was Philip, Lord Wharton. A resounding scandal ensued. The writer of this broadside is of the opinion that these infamies were largely due to 'the Impieties of the late French Prophets', the villains whom D'Urfey exposed in his satirical comedy. Mrs. Delany in her *Autobiography* relates how Dr Friend, the famous Jacobite physician, told some young persons that he had been present at the fearful deathbed of a Mr Howe, who had been a member of this horrible society. The unhappy wretch in the throes of dissolution screamed out with terrific imprecations that he was lost eternally.

Only eight years later, *Hell Upon Earth: Or, The Town in an Uproar*, draws a hideous picture of a satanic sodality which met in a subterranean cellar. The members for the sake of 'wealth and wit' made a secret but overt and formal pact with the demon.

In Ireland one of the vilest and most notorious of these demoniac Societies was the Blasters, whose chief officer the authorities discovered to be Peter Lens, a miniature painter, and a professed Satanist, who openly declared himself a votary of the Devil, whose health he had publicly drunk with such horrid execrations as appalled the Select Committee of the Irish House of Lords, which sat to inquire into these flagrant impieties. A number of persons were examined under oath concerning the dark doings of these 'loose and disorderly' reprobates, but Lens seems to have escaped punishment by absconding and swiftly crossing over to England. Profoundly moved and cut to the very heart, Bishop Berkeley penned a trenchant and timely censure upon the *Enormous License and Irreligion of the Times*, in which he emphasised that the blasphemies of the Blasters were no ordinary profanities or oaths uttered in the debauch of drink or the heat of passion, but a studied, deliberate, and public worship of the Devil.

There exists, in storage in the National Gallery of Ireland, Dublin, a large canvas painted by James Worsdale between 1735–1738 depicting five prominent members, men of the foulest character, of 'The Dublin Hell-Fire Club'. This abominable fraternity was founded by Richard Parsons, first Earl of Rosse, who for some reason does not appear in the picture. The Eagle Tavern on Cork Hill was a frequent meeting-place of these diabolists, but the favourite scene of their iniquities was a hunting-lodge on Mount Pelier, near Rathfarnham, which is seven miles south-west of Dublin. This sequestered and out-of-the-way spot was an odd choice for a building. Erected in the 1720s by the Speaker of the House of Commons, William Conolly, and soon deserted by him, it was popularly known as Conolly's Folly. The ground was ill-omened. It had been badly famed as a rendezvous of sorcerers for many a long year past. Even today it is avoided, and many a dark story is still current of strange eerie happenings in this horribly haunted place. The lodge itself is now a mere ruin, hideous, gaping, and bare, but I think that even so those who have visited it must be conscious of the aura of concentrated evil.

Here, then, the Hell-Fire Club was wont to meet. It is recorded that during these orgies there were actually diabolic manifestations, and familiars materialised. It is said that the seat of the vice-chairman was always left empty, and on occasion it was seen to be occupied by a dark shadowy impalable figure with red fiery eyes.

This 'Damnable Cabal', as it was aptly termed, continued – being carried on by new recruits into the infernal society – for more than fifty years. Indeed, there is evidence that about 1770 a Black Mass was celebrated at the Lodge. In 1779, when Austin Cooper, the antiquary, visited the place he found it in a ruinous condition, but it is believed that during one of the sabbats, not long before, the building had caught fire and was badly damaged. It was said in bitter jest that the votaries of Satan must have deliberately ignited the pile to acclimatise themselves to the eternal furnace, the hell of which they stood in such imminent jeopardy. A wicked sally, but perchance perilously true. At any rate, one is not surprised that even yet the phantoms of the wretched men who revelled there are reported to be doomed and bound to the earthly scene of their devilish crimes, and the spectre of Colonel John St Leger, not the least infamous of this warlock junto, rides abroad (so folk say) at dark midnight in a coach of flame, whose driver, postilions, and coal-black steeds are all headless, a horrible portent of bale.

As in Ireland, so in Scotland, there were impious clubs. Robert Chambers, the antiquary, in his *Traditions of Edinburgh*, 1824, tells how he had talked with grave elderly people who knew the 'last wornout members of such clubs', miserable wretches who, remorseful and repentant, confessed they had once made pacts with Satan. Chambers was credibly assured that many of the clubs or covens were affiliated to the London and Irish fraternities of evil, and that at one time a high official in these devilries used to travel round and visit each cell or centre to 'propagate their vile wickedness'. This demonist fell into a deep melancholy and, reflecting upon the horror of his position, went mad, and died raving. The Scottish clubs had various secret rendezvous in Edinburgh: Allan's Close, Halkerston's Wynd – a wynd is a narrow side-street or passage – and Carrider's Close. The principal scene of their sabbat orgies was in Jack's Close, Canongate. These foul mysteries were celebrated under conditions of almost impenetrable secrecy, and neophytes were obliged to submit to tests of a most horrible and obscene nature before being admitted.

Unfortunately Satanism was practised in the two Universities. As early as 1727 reference is made to a Hell-Fire Club at Oxford. Eighteen years later there was a shocking scandal when that notoriously morbid profligate, George Selwyn, was sent down with public ignominy from Hertford College for assisting at the celebration of a mock-communion in a tavern near St Martin's Church, in High Street. He had mingled the blood from his arm with the contents of the chalice, a piece of witchcraft recalling the infamous eucharist of l'abbé Guibourg in the Palladian chapel of the rue Beauregard.

In spite of the watchfulness of the proctors and other authorities, such is the cunning of diabolism, the foul tradition continued. In the year 1829 a 'Hell-Fire Club', consisting of undergraduate members, assembled twice weekly, generally in the rooms of the President in Brasenose College. This College on the north side is bounded by the narrow passage, known as Brasenose Lane, and this connects with Turl Street, the Square wherein stand the Radcliffe Camera and the main entrance of Brasenose, directly facing All Souls. As one goes down towards the Square from the Turl, on the left-hand side is the high garden wall of Exeter; upon the right, the north portion of Lincoln College, which adjoins Brasenose. The windows of Brasenose which give upon the Lane are of a narrow Jacobean order, heavily barred and protected by horizontal as well as perpendicular stanchions. The lower casements, moreover, being nearly on a level with the causeway, are yet further secured by a stoutly meshed wire netting.

One December midnight in 1829 the Rev. T. T. Churton, a Fellow and Tutor of Brasenose, was returning to his rooms, and having crossed out of the Turl had got more than half-way down the Lane, when he saw a tall person, draped in a long black cloak and wearing a large broad-brimmed sombrero pulled down over his face, apparently helping someone to make his exit by means of the window. Most of the rooms were curtained and in darkness, but from this particular corner there streamed a brilliant light. He at once hurried forward to prevent so flagrant a breach of the College regulations, since this room belonged to a wealthy undergraduate, who was strongly suspected of being one of the leading spirits in the

Hell-Fire Club. As he advanced he was conscious that a violent struggle was in progress, and that the undergraduate, whose features, distorted with an agonising spasm of the most ghastly fear, he clearly recognised, was being literally forced through the bars by the superior strength of the mysterious stranger. For a second Dr Churton caught a glimpse of the latter's countenance, which was so demoniacal and unearthly, so hideous and terrible, that he realised the creature was none other than a fiend of the nether pit. Years after he declared that these appalling lineaments would for ever remain horribly stamped upon his memory. Uttering a prayer for help and strength, he managed to rush past and gained the College gates, upon which he knocked frantically. As the porter opened the door, he collapsed in a deep swoon. At the same moment, with loud cries of wildest alarm and dismay, there trooped out from the rooms immediately to the right of the porter's lodge a crowd of men – the members of the notorious Hell-Fire Club. In the midst of a speech of more than ordinary profanity, with a terrific imprecation upon his lips, the President, who was indeed the owner of these rooms, had fallen dead, and was lying there a convulsed and blackened corpse.

What Dr Churton had seen was more than sufficiently clear. It may be remembered that the grave Tertullian, in his Fifth Book (Chapter xv), *Against Marcion*, gives it as his opinion that 'The soul has a kind of body of a quality peculiar to itself.'

The Hell-Fire Club in question never met again. Early in the present century, in 1912, there was, however, a Hell-Fire Club in Oxford, and in 1930 witchcraft and necromancy were being clandestinely practised in the University. It would appear that the evil traditions of Satanism persisted and were handed on, unbroken, from generation to generation of Undergraduates. (In 1934 a Hell-Fire Club was meeting in London.) Not many years previously a black mass was celebrated abominably in the ruins of Godstow Nunnery, and it was with difficulty that an open scandal was averted. In more than one village churchyard near Oxford the necromancies of Kelley and Paul Waring have been essayed.

Much the same tale might be told of Cambridge, where, it will be remembered, a number of witches were examined by Dr Henry More, the famous seventeenth-century Platonising divine and metaphysician. But it would be tedious to repeat these histories of undergraduate warlockry and impieties.

Of all these profligate and satanical fraternities that coven which has left the most infamous and enduring name is no doubt the sodality known as 'The Monks of Medmenham'.

Sir Francis Dashwood, Lord Le Despenser, the 'Founder and Father' of the Monks, born in 1708, at the age of sixteen inherited vast wealth and estates, including the fair domain of West Wycombe, where his father had built himself a great country house. But the son was by no means content with mere old-fashioned architecture of Vanbrugh's school, however overloaded and grandiose, and he proceeded to turn West Wycombe Park into a mansion, which, even in those days of immense ostentation, ran riot superfluent in a profusion of protuberant porticoes and colonnades, pœciles, loggias, and peristyles, without, all 'in the Grecian gust'; within, most sumptuously Italian, elaborately frescoed, with gaily painted ceilings of amorous foreshortened heroes and gods and goddesses. Gossip has it, be the truth as it may, that of the many gorgeous rooms some few are discreetly kept locked owing to the priapean nature of the decorations and the extraordinary objects of virtu Dashwood collected in his more private cabinets and vitrines.

Only a few miles from West Wycombe Park were the ancient ruins of Medmenham Abbey, an early Cistercian foundation, which, despoliated and desecrated, in the reign of Queen Elizabeth had been purchased from the Crown by the Duffield family, and more or less converted into a dwelling-house or small manor. In 1752 Medmenham was owned by Francis Duffield, a handsome, limber youth who is described as being 'of affable disposition, having large dark blue eyes' (A. H. Plaisted, *The Manor and Parish Records of Medmenham*). Unhappily, he had fallen under the evil influence of Dashwood, and became his devoted acolyte.

As early as 1725, when he was but seventeen, Sir Francis Dashwood was known to be a member of a Hell-Fire Club, which met for its lewd orgies in a secret cellar. It was in this same Society that the libertine and 'universally hated' Lord Sandwich cut so prominent and foul a figure, an enormous profligate, whose life, according to Lord Chesterfield, most lenient and easy-going of observers, was 'one uniform, unblushing course of debauchery and dissipation' from his very teens.

Sir Francis Dashwood, so rumour ran, whilst on the Grand Tour, his first Continental travels, had been initiated into the diabolic cult by a master cabbalist at Venice. Certain it is that he brought back with him from France and Italy a number of grimoires and magical manuals of the most hideous impiety, which could have been obtained in no ordinary way.

To a Satanist, such as he, the foundation of a demoniacal fraternity and the celebration of their goetic ritual in the actual sanctuary where once the Holy Sacrifice had been offered day by day and cowled monks had knelt in penance and in prayer gave something of an extra and exquisite titilation of wickedness he hardly hoped to indulge and enjoy.

In 1752–1753 Medmenham Abbey was rented on a long lease from the Duffields, elaborate alterations were made at great expense, and 'the Friars of St Francis', as they were mockingly dubbed, the Brotherhood, were enrolled, Frank Duffield being one of the first novices.

Exactly what these alterations were can well be imagined, and indeed we have contemporary descriptions of the interior of the Abbey. There was a richly ornate withdrawing-room with long lounging sofas covered with green silk damask; a remarkable refectory, for 'the cellars were stored with the choicest wines, the larders with the delicacies of every climate'; a library, whose shelves were amply supplied with pornographic volumes and obscene engravings; a number of small, but luxuriously appointed, *cells* or bedchambers, for the 'friars', 'fitted up for all the purposes of lasciviousness, for which proper objects were also provided'. As one walked down the corridors spintrian pictures met the eye, paintings of consummate art but of the rankest lubricity. In fine, 'there was not a vice for practising which he [Sir Francis] did not make provision'.

'Thus far', as Charles Johnstone aptly observes, 'the ridicule, however criminal in itself, may seem to have been designed only against those societies of human institution', but the main object was 'to attack the very essentials of Religion', acknowledged by every serious person to be divine. The chapel, the secret shrine of the 'Friars', was the Sanctum Sanctorum of Satanism. This no one was allowed to enter save the Superiors, the inner circle of the elect. 'The decorations', Walpole drily observes, 'may well be supposed to have contained the quintessence of their mysteries, since it was impenetrable to any but the initiated.' That the visitors to Medmenham, and indeed many members of this infamous Society, were lecherous rakehells who assembled for the practice of unbridled lewdness is of course, a fact beyond question, but it is also certain that among the vile there were viler still, 'the elect', or in plain words Satanists, devoted to the worship of the fiend.

In the chapel there was an apsidal sanctuary, balustraded with elaborately carved altar-rail, within which upon the foot-space stood the altar with its candlesticks and furniture, equipped for the celebration of the eucharist of hell. One night the chapel was solemnly dedicated to Satan, in hideous mockery of the Consecration of a Church.

Chiefest among those who formed this 'inner group', pre-sided over by 'Prior Sir Francis' himself, were young Francis Duffield; Lord Sandwich; 'Old Paul' Whitehead, a notorious libertine and something of a satirical poet; George Selwyn, charnelly decadent and debauched; Thomas Potter, a vicious, hard, cynical wit, to whom with some reason has been assigned that pornographic and profane piece *An Essay on Woman*, with which the name of John Wilkes is so intimately and inextric-ably connected. Nor without reason, for even if Wilkes him-self did not write the wretched thing – a 'most scandalous, obscene and impious libel . . . most wicked, and blasphe-mous' the house of Lords justly enough termed it – without a doubt he 'enlarged the sketch', and it was he who was respon-sible for having the type set up and correcting the proofs, although only a dozen copies were intended to have been struck off to be distributed among his cronies, the Friars of Medmenham.

It was to Wilkes, in fact, that the dissolution of the Medmen-ham sodality was mainly due. It has been truly said that 'the Brotherhood of St Francis, like the Roman Empire, decayed from within', but the disbanding was helped on and hastened from without. 'Politics', says Horace Walpole, 'no sooner in-fused themselves amongst these rosy anchorites, than dis-sensions were kindled, and a false brother [John Wilkes] arose, who divulged the arcana, and exposed the good Prior.' Not only were there internecine disputes, but fierce quarrels in the parliamentary arena, when Lord Sandwich in the House of Lords was impeaching Wilkes for blasphemy. The pot calling the kettle black.

At the last meeting of the Friars in June, 1762, only half a dozen members assembled. Not only scandal but indignation was being popularly bruited. The tale of profligacy might be told, but the tale of Satanism must not be so much as whispered, cost what it may. Lampoons and caricatures were appearing. One print, entitled *Secrets of the Convent*, seemed to aim perilously near the truth. The diabolical chapel was stripped of its contents, which were hidden away at West Wycombe Park. Books, paintings, furniture followed.

Medmenham Abbey was deserted. Only a twelvemonth after the final rendezvous of the brethren, in 1763, Horace Walpole found the place 'Very ruinous and bad'. Long before the end of the eighteenth century not a vestige of the Sanctum Sanctorum, the mysterious chapel, was left, and then, having been sold in 1777 by Francis Duffield, the Abbey was leased to quite poor folk, who were eager to earn vails from parties of sightseers by showing them the rooms where the Friars had revelled and roared and raked. An extra tip would elicit melodramatic stories of ghosts and imps and devilkins and bugaboos. Picknickers crowded the sloping lawns on hot summer afternoons.

Today, as ever, the curious still flock to the Abbey; tales are told and the ruins echo to chatter and good humour. But no-one should be deceived, Sir Francis and his Friars may be no more, but elsewhere their descendants in Satan's service are abroad and evil, degeneracy and corruption flourish in his name...

MARY SHELLEY

Mary Shelley (née Mary Wollstonecraft Godwin) was born in Somers Town, London, in 1797. She came from rich literary heritage; her father was the political philosopher William Godwin, and her mother was the philosopher and feminist Mary Wollstonecraft. In 1812, when she was just fifteen, Mary met the poet Percy Bysshe Shelley. Shelley was married at the time, but the two spent the summer of 1814 travelling around Europe together. In 1815, Mary gave birth prematurely to a girl, and the infant died twelve days later. In her journal of March 19, 1815, Mary recorded a nightmare she'd had, now cited as a possible inspiration for her future masterwork, *Frankenstein*: "Dream that my little baby came to life again - that it had only been cold & that we rubbed it before the fire & it lived."

In the summer of 1816, the couple famously visited the poet Lord Byron at his villa beside Lake Geneva, in Switzerland. Storms and tumultuous weather (common in Shelley's future novel) confined them to the indoors, where they and Byron's assorted other guests took to reading to each other from a book of ghost stories. One evening, Byron challenged all his guests to write one themselves. The guests obliged, and Mary's story went on to become *Frankenstein*. Mary and Percy married later that year, and eighteen months later, in 1818 *Frankenstein* was published. Mary was only 21, and the novel was a huge success. The first edition of the book included a preface from Percy, and many, disbelieving that a young woman could have penned such a horror story, thought that the novel was his.

In 1819, following the death of another child, Mary suffered a nervous breakdown. This was compounded three years later when her husband drowned. Widowed at just 25, Mary returned to England, determined to continue profiting from her writing in order to support her one surviving son. Between 1827 and 1840, she was busy as an author and editor, penning three more novels and a number of short stories. However, she never experienced further success of the sort that *Frankenstein* had brought. Her final decade was blighted by illness, and throughout the 1840s she suffered from terrible headaches and bouts of paralysis in parts of her body. In 1851, at Chester Square, she died at the age of fifty-three from what her physician suspected was a brain tumour.

Shelley underwent a period of critical neglect after her death, due in part to the onset of the realist movement. For a long time she was chiefly remembered as the wife of Percy Bysshe Shelley, and it was not until 1989 that a full-length scholarly biography was published. In recent decades, the republication of almost all her writing, including her short fiction, has stimulated a new recognition of its value, and scholars now consider Mary Shelley to be a major figure in Romanticism.

ALPHONSE DAUDET

Alphonse Daudet was born in Nimes, France in 1841. After a difficult boyhood, and an abandoned career in schoolteaching, he left home for Paris aged just sixteen in the hope of becoming a writer. His first collection of poems, *Les Amoureuses* (1858), was well-received by critics, and Daudet began writing plays. He was appointed secretary to Morny, one of Napoleon Bonaparte's most powerful ministers, and Daudet found himself with much free time to write. His 1872 novel *Tartarin de Tarascon* was a major success, as was *Fromont Jeune et Risler Aîné* (1874). *Jack* (1876) cemented his reputation, and Daudet spent the rest of his life as a man of letters, penning some twelve more novels and plays. He died in Paris, France in 1897, aged 57.

Alexander Pushkin

Alexander Sergeyevich Pushkin was born in Moscow, Russia in 1799. Hailing from a family of Russian nobles, he was educated at the prestigious Imperial Lyceum, where he published his first poem at the age of fifteen. After graduating, he became part of the vibrant and intellectual youth culture of the then-capital, St. Petersburg, and published his first long poem, *Rusian and Lyudmila* (1820).

Barely into his twenties, Pushkin was already recognised as a major literary talent. However, in 1820, having became vocally committed to radical social reform, he was exiled from the Russian capital by the ruling Tsar. After observing and actively backing the early stages of the Greek Revolution (1821-1832), Pushkin moved to Chișinău (now Moldova, then part of the Russian Empire). Here, he penned two long Romantic poems which brought him wide and major acclaim: *The Captive of the Caucasus* and *The Fountain of Bakhchisaray.* Over the next few years, forever under the watchful eye of government censors, Pushkin drifted within the Russian Empire. In 1825, while living at his mother's rural estate in Odessa (now Ukraine, then part of the Russian Empire), he penned what has become his most famous play, *Boris Godunov.* However, it took him six years to publish it, and forty years to get it approved by censors and staged.

Between 1825 and 1832, Pushkin's famous novel in verse, *Eugene Onegin,* was serialized. Now a classic of Russian letters, its eponymous protagonist has served as the model for numerous other Russian literary heroes. In 1831, he met another future great of Russian literature, Nikolai Gogol, and helped publicize much of his work. However, just six years later, the notoriously short-tempered Pushkin challenged a man who had been courting his wife to a duel. The encounter left the Russian mortally wounded, and he died two days later, in February of 1837, aged just 37.

Pushkin's legacy is vast; he is now widely considered to be the greatest Russian poet of all time, and the founder of modern Russian literature. His last home is now a much-visited museum in central St. Petersburg.

M. R. James

Montague Rhodes James was born in Kent, England in 1862. An intellectually gifted child, he excelled academically at both Temple Grove School and Eton College before enrolling at King's College, Cambridge. A highly respected scholar to this day, James' areas of research interest were apocryphal Biblical literature and mediaeval illuminated manuscripts. He was, by turns, Fellow, Dean, and Tutor at King's College, and in 1905 was installed as Provost. James was a highly sociable man, and he travelled widely throughout Europe.

James came to writing fiction relatively late, not publishing his first collection of short stories – *Ghost Stories of an Antiquary* (1904) – until the age of 42. Many of his tales were written as Christmas Eve entertainments and read aloud to friends. James described his introduction to ghosts in 1931: "In my childhood I chanced to see a toy Punch and Judy set, with figures cut out in cardboard. One of these was The Ghost. It was a tall figure habited in white with an unnaturally long and narrow head, also surrounded with white, and a dismal visage. Upon this my conceptions of a ghost were based, and for years it permeated my dreams." James believed that must a good story must "put the reader into the position of saying to himself: 'If I'm not careful, something of this kind may happen to me!'" He eventually published five collections of his ghost stories, all of which were reprinted and adapted numerous times.

Modern scholars now see James as having redefined the ghost story for the 20th century by abandoning many of the formal Gothic clichés of his predecessors and using more realistic contemporary settings. However, James's tales tend to reflect his own antiquarian interests, and he is seen as the founder of the 'antiquarian ghost story'. His first two collections – *Ghost Stories of an Antiquary* (1904) and *More Ghost Stories* (1911) – are generally regarded as his most important, containing as they do the well-known stories 'Number 13', 'Count Magnus', 'Oh, Whistle and I'll Come to You, My Lad' and 'Casting the Runes'.

The onset of World War One marked the beginning of the end of James' golden years in Cambridge. In 1918, he accepted the post of Provost of Eton College. He was awarded the Order of Merit in 1930, and died in 1936, aged 73.

THOMAS PREST

Thomas Peckett Prest was born in 1810. Originally a talented musician and composer, Prest made a name for himself as a highly prolific producer of 'penny dreadfuls' – a Victorian era publishing trend of lurid and sensationalist stories printed over a series of weeks on cheap pulp paper. His most famous co-creation was the 'demon barber' Sweeney Todd, made famous by the story originally titled *The String of Pearls.* He is also thought to be the possible of author of *Varney the Vampire.* Prest died in 1859.

JOHN WILLIAM POLIDORI

John William Polidori was born in London, England in 1795. In 1810, he enrolled at the University of Edinburgh, where he wrote a thesis on sleepwalking and graduated as a doctor of medicine. In 1816, Polidori entered Lord Byron's service as his personal physician, accompanying him through Europe and keeping a diary of their travels. After parting ways with Byron, he travelled through Italy before returning to England, and in April of 1819, his story 'The Vampyre' was published in *New Monthly Magazine*. The story is now seen as a progenitor of the romantic vampire genre of fantasy fiction, and the first vampire story ever published in English. Suffering from depression and gambling debts, Polidori died two years after its appearance, possibly via suicide, aged just 25.

MRS. HUGH FRASER

Mary Crawford Fraser – better-known by her pen name, Mrs. Hugh Fraser – was born in Italy in 1851.Orphaned at a young age, Fraser was raised in various locations throughout Europe, and attended boarding school on the Isle of Wight.In 1874, she married a diplomat, and followed him to his postings in Peking, Vienna, Rome, Santiago and Tokyo.Although she was left a widow twenty years later, the global travels inspired Fraser, and in the 1890s she turned to writing.Over the rest of her life, she produced a string of predominately historical novels, the best-known being *Palladia* (1896), *The Looms of Time* (1898), *The Stolen Emperor* (1904), *A Diplomatist's Wife in Japan* (1912) and *Italian Yesterdays* (1913).Fraser died In 1922.

CHARLES MATURIN

Charles Maturin was born in Dublin, Ireland in 1782. He was educated at Trinity College, Dublin and became Anglican Curate of St. Peter's Church in Dublin in 1803, one year before marrying his wife, ell-known singer Henrietta Kingsbury.

Maturin's first three novels were produced under a pseudonym, Dennis Jasper Murphy, and were both critical and financial flops. However, Maturin was spotted by Sir Walter Scott, who introduced Lord Byron to Maturin's work, and under their direction Maturin turned to play-writing. In 1816, Maturin's *Bertram* opened in the West End, and was a great success, drawing a wide audience and running for 22 nights. However, Maturin continued to suffer from financial hardship, and to make matters worse, *Bertram* was denounced as almost atheistic by Samuel Taylor Coleridge. This, combined with his reputation for eccentricity, dandyism, and a love of dancing and theatre, prevented Maturin from further clerical advancement.

Maturin continued trying to support himself financially through writing, with mixed success. In 1820, he produced his best-known work, the novel *Melmoth the Wanderer*. Considered by many critics to be the last traditional Gothic novel, after his death the work became a great success. In France – where somewhat oddly Maturin achieved a readership far greater than he ever did in Ireland – Honoré de Balzac, Charles Baudelaire and Victor Hugo all expressed their deep admiration for the novel. Similarly, speaking almost a century later, H. P. Lovecraft called it "an enormous stride in the evolution of the horror-tale." Maturin died in 1824.

MONTAGUE SUMMERS

Augustus Montague Summers was born in Bristol,
England in 1880. He was raised as an evangelical
Anglican in a wealthy family, and studied at Clifton
College before reading theology at Trinity College,
Oxford with the intention of becoming a Church of
England priest. In 1905, he graduated with fourth-
class honours, and went on to continue his religious
training at the Lichfield Theological College. Summers
entered his apprenticeship as a curate in the diocese of
Bitton near Bristol, but rumours of an interest in
Satanism and accusations of sexual misconduct with
young boys led to him being cut off; a scandal which
dogged him his whole life. Summers joined the

growing ranks of English men of letters interested in medievalism and the occult. In 1909, he converted to Catholicism and shortly thereafter he began passing himself off as a Catholic priest, the legitimacy of which was disputed. Around this time, Summers adopted a curious attire which included a sweeping black cape and a silver-topped cane.

Summers eventually managed to make a living as a full-time writer. He was interested in the theatre of the seventeenth century, particularly that of the English Restoration, and was one of the founder members of The Phoenix, a society that performed neglected works of that era. In 1916, he was elected a fellow of the Royal Society of Literature. Summers also produced some important studies of Gothic fiction. However, his interest in the occult never waned, and in 1928, around the time he was acquainted with Aleister Crowley, he published the first English translation of Heinrich Kramer and James Sprenger's *Malleus Maleficarum* ('*The Hammer of Witches*'), a

15th century Latin text on the hunting of witches. Summers then turned to vampires, producing *The Vampire: His Kith and Kin* (1928) and *The Vampire in Europe* (1929), and then to werewolves with *The Werewolf* (1933). Summers' work on the occult is known for his unusual, archaic writing style, his intimate style of narration, and his purported belief in the reality of the subjects he treats.

In his day, Summers was a renowned eccentric; *The Times* called him "in every way a 'character'" and "a throwback to the Middle Ages." He died at his home in Richmond, Surrey.

www.ingramcontent.com/pod-product-compliance
Lightning Source LLC
Chambersburg PA
CBHW030342030726
47499CB00003B/876